CAROLINA'S HANDBOOK ON SUMMONING

BOOK THREE OF THE DRC FILES

KEVIN A DAVIS

Inkd
Publishing

For my Family

CAROLINA'S HANDBOOK ON SUMMONING

CONTENTS

CHAPTER
ONE

On the last day of the conference, Miranda Powell spoke with a seasoned ease to an audience of well-dressed accountants, financial advisers, and others interested in her fiscal speculations of the present economy based on her tenure as a member of the Department of International Economic Affairs. However, it was her years as a judge that allowed her to appear calm despite the threat against her life and the three security guards who accompanied her.

Two of their team were witches. She'd never had any direct interest in the arcane nor any inherent abilities, but her work with the Consociation reached back decades to when she'd been a defense lawyer.

She placed both her palms on the cool wood of the podium, made a slight joke, and smiled as the audience murmured with some appreciation. The large window behind her lit their faces better than the lights on the high ceiling. The room at the convention center had a foul smell rising in it, but she had the professional acumen not to let it show on her face.

One of her guards, a bodybuilder from his figure, appeared to have less control as he shifted, sniffing the air with a distasteful expression. The one to her right remained motionless and inscrutable, though his reddish hair seemed out of place for their profession. Why she thought that, she didn't take the time to ponder. The third guard had more of the appearance she expected with a shaved face, short dark hair, and steely eyes that watched the backs of her audience from the far wall by the exit doors. The videographer beside the black jacketed sentinel had a full beard and the youthful appearance of an artisan, despite his blue suit.

It was he, as he gawked to her left, who alerted her to the attack.

Miranda's words died in her throat when she saw the woman embracing her guard from behind. Long black hair covered her face, and her naked skin had the gray pallor of the dead, but the body had a firm, youthful appearance.

One arm held her body tight against the guard's back while the other reached around as if for his face. The moment he began to react and struggle, bright blood sprayed the stunned audience. The attacker held a blood-covered silver blade, which she raised triumphantly. Then she turned bright, intense eyes toward Miranda. Her mouth opened in a smile and her tongue appeared to squirm.

The guard dropped forward, knees hitting the floor first. His head landed in the lap of a drenched man in what had been a pristine, navy pin-striped suit. The skull bent impossibly back so that the guard's dead, shocked eyes stared up at the man in the folding chair, then the corpse locked there, pressed forward by the weight of his body.

The audience screamed, almost as one. The man with the dead security guard in his lap fell backward, and chairs clattered like dominoes. Those on the outer edges leaped in a shrieking run for the exit doors.

The gray woman faced Miranda. Her arms painted with bright red made her appear more alive. She wore a white amulet on her chest that sparkled in the light coming from the huge windows behind the stage.

Miranda had taken the death threat seriously, as she always did. What she hadn't expected was that her assassin would be dead. She never questioned the Consociation about details of magic or the cryptids, but she'd helped in situations that leaked rumors of undead creatures, or even werewolves.

As the uproar filled the room, the dead woman leaped unnaturally onto the stage. Thick blood dropped from the silver blade.

Panic tightened her chest, but Miranda could only stumble backward.

The attacker moved a step, appearing to enjoy Miranda's fear. The smile and the disturbing churning inside the dark mouth continued.

The audience roiled around fallen chairs to Miranda's right, and she considered joining the fray. She spun to find the red-headed guard climbing the stage to protect her. Spinning, Miranda took two quick steps across the hollow wood and leaped off to join him.

She had no idea if he were one of the witches who protected her, but she knew they had guns. What that might do against someone already dead, she didn't know.

The man barely let Miranda land before he wrapped an arm around her and practically lifted her to run in the direction of the far wall, away from the crowd, the exit doors, and the assassin. When she saw the single maintenance door ahead, she sped in earnest.

She squandered a quick glance behind. The assassin

had disappeared, but the crowd had stampeded the door. They were pounding against it and crushing each other. The bedlam echoing in the room had gone from high-pitched shrieks to angry howling. The third member of the security team had his weapon out and ran nearly sideways toward her, watching the room.

The assassin was gone.

Miranda focused on the door ahead. Her guard let her go as they reached it, and he turned the knob, but the door didn't budge.

Miranda's racing heart stopped as she spun to study the room. The crowd had frayed. Some thudded and yelled at the doors while some just crumpled and sobbed at the walls. Others had split off, running toward her, but they slowed as she didn't exit. One of those knocked down the videographer's tripod. Sound faded into a thudding echo, and she feared her heart might fail. The bearded artisan noticed the fallen camera and broke from the crowd to retrieve it.

Her other guard arrived. "Shoot the lock. Step behind me, ma'am."

Numb, she moved to comply and smelled the foul odor once again. Even as she opened her mouth to speak, the woman appeared out of nowhere and stabbed at Miranda. Something invisible held the silver blade a foot from Miranda's chest. Her breath frozen in her throat, she stumbled back.

The dead assassin snarled and lashed at the red-haired man without a glance. He'd been reaching for his weapon, but she gutted him with a cut from one hip to the other. Intestines rolled from the gash in his white, buttoned-down shirt. Pink and fatty, they tumbled down his black slacks to his polished shoes. They seemed endless.

The gunshot shocked Miranda back to focus.

The last security guard had shot the assassin. The impact turned the woman's torso, but her feet and head remained oddly facing forward, so she twisted at the hips. A neat black hole showed in the gray skin just above her left breast. Tiny legs squirmed at the edge of the wound. The assassin lunged half sideways at the security guard.

A dull report of a second shot echoed in Miranda's ears as she took another hesitant step in retreat.

The man fell back with the assassin on top of him. A dark, scrambling mass crawled up his shirt and jacket. Black bugs swarmed across him.

Terror locked his implacable face as the wave broke over his neck and chin. He might have been screaming in the deafening silence, but Miranda could see the bugs crawl into his mouth. They reached his eyes as the assassin's silver blade plunged into the swarm on his face.

Miranda nearly fell, her limbs became so weak in her disgust. Instead, she took a shaky step back. Her ears rung with the last gunshot, and she would have gagged at the stench if she'd been able to breathe.

The assassin turned to peer up at her from under black hair. The blade was still in the guard's head and firmly in her grip. The bugs had become a seething mass that coated him.

Something inside Miranda made her run. She hadn't consciously taken the first step, but once she started, she sprinted for the crowd. It didn't matter that they couldn't get out. They were safer than standing with the assassin, the two dead guards, the bugs, and that silver blade.

The audience had strewn the chairs and even bent some. They heaved against the doors in a unified attempt to break them. A few people were hurt, crawling away from the chaos, but Miranda charged right for them.

Two men wearing blood-splattered polos seemed to be

considering heading toward her, but they'd likely seen the massacre at the service door.

Miranda reached the first chair and wound around it, stepped over the next, then got tangled in the third. Her throat was raw, as if she might be screaming. A frantic glance told her the assassin wasn't close, but she'd been invisible until she struck. Freed from the legs of the chair, she dodged to the left, then swerved around a cluster of them.

Miranda nearly stumbled into the assassin, the dead woman stood so close. The stench of death seeped from her. A cluster of those tiny black bugs scattered over her gray skin near the gunshot wound. The amulet sparkled in the light of the massive windows.

Something tugged at her stomach when Miranda tried to retreat. The assassin's right hand was there, holding the hilt of the blade. She smiled, bugs crawling from between her lips.

Knees weak, Miranda tried to step back, but her legs just kept bending, and the blade ripped at her skin as she slid to the floor. A chair leg caught her shoulder and she rolled slightly, but landed on her back.

The assassin followed her down, straddling Miranda as the pain intensified in her stomach. A short breath brought the stench of decay.

With casual precision, the dead woman cut through Miranda's blouse and yanked her shirt from the waistband of her slacks, exposing her. Bugs crawled on Miranda's bare stomach.

The assassin flipped the knife in her hand, as if it were a pen, and began cutting marks onto Miranda's chest. Miranda tried to stop it, but her arms were weak and her mind frozen in horror. The sharp pain made her breathe in, then she snapped her mouth and eyes shut as she felt tiny legs scampering up her neck. The woman's slices were long and sweeping, then short and precise.

Hands to her face, Miranda whimpered as the bugs climbed in her nose, then sobbed, taking in a deep breath of them. As she choked and the woman held her down, the pain ebbed into unconsciousness.

CHAPTER

TWO

I climbed the creaking, weather-worn steps, eying the recently built carport that housed a shiny new red truck with tires so big they threatened to raise the vehicle too high for the metal roof. The house appeared ready to fall apart with the stairs and porch yielding under my weight.

The doorbell didn't work, so I rapped crisply on the peeling brown paint. A television murmured inside. Dogs barked from behind the building, and I watched the sides carefully. The dirt yard had fragrant pine trees and a vine-covered rusted blue car at the edge of the nearby woods.

A hefty man wearing shorts and a black Led Zeppelin t-shirt opened the door, motioning me in without a greeting. The house smelled like weed.

"Special Agent Kristen Winters," I said, showing him the badge I had ready.

"Yep." The father, based on his age, had short brown hair and a matching mustache on a round face. "Greg's in his room."

The dogs continued to bark from the back of the house

as he closed the door behind me. The striking contrast between old and newly purchased continued in the living area. The ceiling, walls, and floors appeared dingy and ready to peel away while a huge black leather couch faced a massive wall-sized television with a larger-than-life talking head news show. Those, and a banner on the wall with the same logo as his t-shirt, were all sparkling new.

Van, the merfolk agent for the DRC whom I'd replaced, had died during an interview in a place just like this. However, he'd already been here to visit Greg, so I doubted I was in any danger.

He dropped back into his couch as I approached the room he'd gestured to. I tapped on it gently to avoid a fist-sized hole in the hollow door.

"Just go in," the father said. The dogs were still barking.

I hesitated, glancing at the back of the double-wide just to give Greg a moment before I opened the door. The kitchen too had been partially refurnished with a modern stainless-steel fridge and stove contrasting the ratty sink and cabinets.

"Come in," Greg said from inside the room.

His spine had been damaged at the rave, and according to the reports, he couldn't use his legs. There were more surgeries scheduled. I opened the door to his bedroom and found him facing me, seated in a semi-reclined electric wheelchair. Greg had a wall-sized television as well, though his held a paused game. The room wasn't very big, so his bed and chair took up most of the space.

"Hi, Greg." I shifted the door closed behind me, unsure where to stand. "Special Agent Kristen Winters."

"Hi. They said you were coming. I took a couple extra gabapentin. You know. For nerves." Greg Starr had shaved his head so that his dark eyebrows dominated his thin face. He gestured toward the bed for me to sit. "Sorry you had to come out on Sunday. This still upsets Ma, but she's at church all day today."

I had wondered why he was only available today and in the morning. Gingerly, I sat at the edge of his bed, sinking into the mattress. Not wanting to put my hands on his blanket, I tapped at my curls, then folded my fingers in my lap. "Thanks for taking the time."

Greg scoffed. "Nothing else to do." He jabbed a thumb at the frozen game. "Except to play — and it gets old."

Greg already fit one of my criteria since he came from a low-income family. I wanted to see if the same woman had invited him who had met with Joe Capra, the first victim of the rave I had interviewed. Van had been focused on the DJ's assistant.

"I'll try to keep this brief and not dwell too much on what's already in the report." I flashed a smile. "How did you find out about the rave? Were you invited?"

"Yeah. Kal told me about it." Greg's lips flattened. Kal had died at the rave in Jacksonville; a friend of Greg's, according to the reports. They had gone down to visit the beaches. "He was the one who sucker punched me, for no reason."

"Did someone invite him?"

"Don't know."

"How did he find out about the rave, did he say?"

"No." Greg rubbed his hand over his scalp. His lips pursed, as if he stopped from saying something. "The other agent asked about beetles. They were throwing something up front, but we were in the back. I couldn't see the DJ or anyone. We weren't even faced that way."

I couldn't be sure if Greg held anything back, or if he just had difficulty talking about the incident. Maybe I could determine which, if I drew him into the story from a different direction. "Okay. Well, you and Kal get to the parking lot of the rave; did you drive together? What do you see?"

"We had Kal's Corolla. There were trucks and people."

"Did you hang outside? What did you do?"

Again, his lips flinched. "We didn't stay in the parking lot very long."

I leaned forward, elbows on knees. "Nothing that you two did caused this. Anything you say isn't going anywhere except to help us get to the bottom of who did make this happen. You can tell me anything."

Greg shrugged. "I know. I just figure if you think I was hallucinating it means I didn't know what was going on."

Well, that would be true. "You were hallucinating, both of you?"

"We hit some candy in the car. We didn't double drop or anything."

Candy might mean MDMA, which would cause hallucinations. "Understood. What did you see — hallucinate?"

"You know the white fog they use at these things?"

"Yes." The reports mentioned light use of a fog machine. Consociation techs had analyzed the contents and found nothing but vegetable glycerin.

The dogs were still barking outside. Greg paused as if he might not continue, then took a deep breath before speaking. "I saw a dark fog coming up from the bar area, and it had a face in it."

A chill ran up my spine. Greg wouldn't know that what he was describing could be a jinn or the transforming of a demon. Van's speculation had been focused on the DJ's assistant, Shoo, who'd supposedly been throwing beetles into the crowd. His guess had been that Shoo might have been a demon. This new information didn't fully support his theory, but Greg might have been hallucinating.

"Did Kal see it?"

Greg closed his eyes. "Don't know. I tapped him to show it to him. That's when he clocked me. Knocked me out cold." Tears were forming.

"Hey. No one was able to control themselves. It wasn't your fault or Kal's."

He drew in a deep breath. "Who then?" Greg swallowed. "I know I'm not supposed to ask. Never mind. Pa can't lose the settlement money and go back to working at the chicken mill. I didn't ask, okay?"

I discarded the anxiety the suggestion of a jinn brought and straightened, composing myself at his discomfort. "Don't worry. I won't say anything. But, I am trying to find out what happened. I hope that helps. Can you give me any detail about the face you saw in the gray smoke?"

Whatever we did find out, he'd never be told. The answers to his questions would haunt him. I did hope his surgery allowed him to walk again. He didn't deserve this. One of the victims was still in a coma from the beating they'd taken.

When I left Greg Starr's house, the victim had been sitting forlornly in his wheelchair, the father never said a word as I let myself out, and the dogs were still barking. I'd gained more than I had with Joe Capra's interview. The data points weren't overlapping, but they gave me additional areas to consider for upcoming witnesses. Kal and Greg's schedule the day prior to the rave left plenty of openings for Kal to meet the mystery woman.

My old Chevy Cavalier rumbled to life, and the scent of its exhaust drifted through my open window. It had begun to smell musty. I needed a new air freshener.

I mapped out the hour and a half drive back to my

apartment and considered an audiobook, but I wanted to mull what I'd learned. Without an active case, Marie had given us the day off from the office in the FBI building in Atlanta. I frowned at the list of back roads I would be taking, many of them for only a couple of miles. Greg lived west of Atlanta, nearly in Alabama. The road I pulled onto hadn't even had a drive-by from Google maps yet; I'd checked from the office before I left.

Van had been focused on Shoo, so there might be something with the assistant, if we ever found him. I still couldn't be sure the agent's death had anything to do with his investigation of the case, except that the explosion had happened during his interview with a victim of the rave who had been left a quadriplegic. Her father had shown plenty of signs of being distraught over the situation, but Marie had not closed Van's case. My dragon-shifter boss had been searching for some connection back to the rave, or the ancient witch Iliodor, but she considered Iliodor a suspect in everything.

When I reached I-20, the driving went a lot quicker, and the traffic wasn't bad until I turned onto I-85 in downtown Atlanta. That's when Tomas called my phone, which I didn't expect. My chest tightened. The DRC team's merfolk tech would have been home with his family unless we had a case.

He swore in his high-pitched tone when I answered. "Turn on your damn comms." Tomas hung up.

Swearing a little more delicately, I fumbled open my purse on the passenger seat. Gratefully, the traffic had leveled to a slow but steady trickle through the downtown area. I checked my phone and saw I was half an hour from my apartment.

Sliding the bud into my ear, I tapped it active and caught Finn, the other witch on the DRC team, driving as well from the background noise. He wasn't from the south originally, but he and his husband had lived in Atlanta long enough that he had a hint of the accent. "Pyre, I'll be there in eight minutes. I can pull ammo and grab go bags."

"Okay. David's pulling the reports off the printer now. Tomas, what's Kristen's ETA?"

"Thirty-three minutes, Pyre." His voice made him sound like a ten-year-old boy rather than a merfolk who could have been a century old, for all I knew.

"I —"

Marie cut me off, not realizing I was on the comms. "Have her go directly to the airport and meet us there." She and David were back to full health after their disturbing, bone-shattering interaction with the Mahakala Quartz.

"I'm on the comms," I said. "I'll park at the airport and meet you there. Where are we headed?" I would have sped if I could have.

"Winston-Salem, North Carolina." She made a muffled noise like shushing. "I've got to go, Tibby." Marie's voice became loud again. "Hurry, Kristen. We might still have an active aggressor. Wheels up in forty."

"What's the case?" I asked.

David, the snarkiest member of our team and a vampire, responded in his light-hearted manner. "Dead speaker at a seminar, along with her three guards. Quite grisly from the reports. I'm looking forward to the video."

Grisly could describe a lot of our cases. When did a speaker have guards? I wanted to ask, but they sounded busy.

"Reports are done," David said. "In folders when you come out, Pyre." They'd be at the office. Marie would be in her back room where we usually met to go over a case.

David would be in the front with our desks and the printer. "I'll grab the go bags," he added.

I tensed. David had yet to notice my go bag with the Supernatural patch. I'd managed to keep it hidden and had planned to buy something more appropriate. Finn had said he'd get the bags, but mentioning it would only encourage David to be curious.

Over David's comms, the cabinet squeaked open. Then came the rustle of fabric and a thud, a second, then David's snort. "My Kristen's a fangirl!" He chuckled and continued with an all too sexy voice. "Who is it? I'm up for Dean, but you seem more like a Sam."

I rolled my eyes, but not too much for the heavy Atlanta afternoon traffic. David would play with this topic no matter what I said. Ignoring him, I tried to place Winston-Salem in my mental map — somewhere north of Georgia.

CHAPTER

THREE

I found a spot to park beside the team's Jeep near the small private flights building. I jogged across the parking lot, grateful that it hadn't gotten too hot in Atlanta yet. The sharp scent of petroleum wafted in the light breeze.

Inside was empty except for a pale young man at the counter. "I'm with them." Outside the windows, Finn waited for me on the tarmac outside the ramp of the Consociation's small jet plane.

The attendant gave me a cursory glance, seemed unimpressed by my curvy figure, and sniffed as if he didn't care. They didn't treat me like that when I was with Marie.

I slammed out the door. "Thanks."

Finn was beaming as I trotted toward him. He nudged his head toward the plane and his dreads swung. "David loves your go bag."

My face flushed as I slowed and let him lead the way. He was six feet tall, athletically built for nearing fifty years old, and had rich brown skin. Of all the team, he'd adopted me as his friend from the first day.

"I kept meaning to replace it." My breathing heavy from the exertion, I tried not to sound embarrassed.

"Too late. We might as well enjoy the show now." He motioned me up the steps in front of him.

The jet had four oversized seats, a fifth that dropped down in the back, and a tiny bathroom. The cabinets held a fridge and even a coffee maker. On my seat sat a tan folder, which would have the printed preliminary reports of the case.

Marie, as curvy as me with a shaved head, sat across from where I would sit. Her sharp dragon-shifter eyes peered at me as I bustled into my chair.

"Thirty-two minutes — to the parking lot." I flashed a smile, ignoring David.

Black haired, handsome, and impeccably dressed, he leered from his seat across the aisle from Marie. The jet seemed large and luxurious, but small at the same time. David slid my hidden go bag from beside his legs, grinning wide enough to show sharp cuspids.

Marie caught my expression as I froze, midway to buckling myself in. She frowned at David. "Stow it — and I mean literally."

The engines were winding up, and the crew closed the door. David stood and headed for the small storage closet, flashing the patch on my bag as he carried it. He asked, "What does a sad cowboy and a Supernatural fan have in common?"

I blushed and hid my smile. My love of good puns had come from my dad, but I wasn't about to answer that in front of Marie.

Finn rescued me. "We have video? I heard David mention something."

Tomas piped in over the comms, "Ready when you are. I have a fairly good video from someone at the seminar, but trouble getting anything decent from the conference center security. Glitches on their end."

Marie had her folder open and picked through the sheets. "We'll get to it once we take off. At 1:10 p.m. Miranda Powell and her three guards were attacked by a naked gray woman with a knife. There were sixty-one witnesses attending the seminar. Local FBI are on site at the conference center in Winston-Salem and have cordoned off all exits. Of the witnesses, twenty-nine were sequestered by the FBI; eight have been transported to the hospital; one is dead, crushed at the doors; and twenty-three left prior to local enforcement arrival.

"Night storms, what a mess. All employees accounted for and on premises except for one guard in the hospital who is not expected to live. He was trampled when he opened the doors to the conference room. They'd been blocked from the outside with door jammers.

"Multiple witnesses concur that the attacker disappeared and reappeared unnaturally. The woman did not attack any of the attendees or the videographer. She was last seen carving on Miranda Powell's chest."

The jet started taxiing, and I forced down my apprehension. I didn't like flying and less so in something so small. I fumbled my reports open, trying to catch up.

Finn leafed through his papers. "The descriptions of the attacker are vague. It could be a zombie or a revenant. If it's a zombie, we've got a rogue witch and Consociation-proscribed magic. A revenant might be worse because that means we could have someone letting in something from the Tarus realm."

"A witch," I said, "because the zombie targeted the guards and the speaker. One witness states he was running slightly behind the speaker when the gray woman appeared and gutted her. A witch could coordinate Haven realm magic to create invisibility to mask her zombie." Invisibility was a difficult Haven spell, which I'd never mastered. "A very skilled witch."

The wheels lifted off the tarmac, and I suppressed a shudder. At least the weather was clear and sunny with almost no wind, so turbulence would be minimal.

"Agreed," said Marie. "Tomas, ETA to site?" She had lowered the table between me and herself to bring up the onboard laptop.

"With driving time, 3:12 p.m., Pyre. Local FBI have vests and a vehicle waiting for you at the terminal."

"Thanks, Tomas. Get Leah on a flight to Winston-Salem. She's in Maryland at the moment. We're going to need extra hands."

"Got it, Pyre." Tomas's tone was less than enthusiastic.

"Leah?" I asked.

Marie powered up the laptop. "You almost met her in Tallahassee. Ready for video, Tomas."

I remembered the name, but had forgotten about her. She'd been called to help, but I'd figured out who had the Mahakala Quartz by then.

"Feed up, Pyre."

I shifted toward the aisle as Marie faced it there for David and Finn. An older woman with silver hair stood at the podium facing a crowd of seated attendees with their backs to the camera. A security guard stood at each side of the podium.

"Why did she have security?" David asked.

"Death threats," Finn answered.

I'd seen the report. Miranda had been a judge at one point and a government official for a previous administration.

The first attack happened so quickly that Marie paused the video and rewound, then reduced the speed to play again. The guard who died never saw his attacker. The zombie had a weapon the size of a hunting knife, but silver through the hilt. She slit his throat before he could react. When she appeared to the camera, we could only see her gray arms as one wrapped across his chest and the other brought the weapon to his throat.

I didn't see her face and body until he fell forward. She had been young, possibly late twenties with a fit figure, now gray-skinned, and long dark hair. The only thing she wore was a sparkling white amulet on a long chain.

Marie paused the video. "Have you identified, Tomas?"

"That's the White Diamond Periapt," Finn said.

Tomas sounded perturbed. "He's right. I've got a good quality zoom of it, and I've matched it point for point. Consociation database lists the item as possibly under Iliodor's control."

"I know." Marie nearly growled. She resumed the video, and the zombie turned to face Miranda, her obvious target.

The audience had begun to react with shrieks, and some jumped from their seats, blocking the camera's view. I could only make out the stage and the dark hair of the zombie.

"Do we have an ID on the zombie yet?" Finn asked.

Tomas swore, lightly for him. "No match yet, but I've had the program running for eighteen minutes."

People screamed and crashed chairs in the audience in a lower-than-expected pitch with the slower playback speed. A man in a pale blue suit blocked our view for a moment, and I expected the camera to get knocked aside. The zombie jumped threateningly onto the stage, and when Miranda escaped at the opposite side of the platform to a waiting security guard, the attacker disappeared. Marie gestured. "White Diamond Periapt."

I glanced at Finn. The database was huge. I couldn't know every talisman.

"Arcane Haven — creates invisibility," Finn explained.

As Miranda and her guard disappeared off the video, Marie paused. "Miranda Powell has been working with the Consociation for decades. She isn't arcane or witch, though. Two of the three-man security force were witches. Adept."

"Which ones?" I asked.

"The two you've seen, from their descriptions. Tomas?"

"Confirmed, Pyre."

She resumed the video, adjusting to real time as we saw nothing, but the shrieking and screaming had risen to a normal pitch. I waited as the last of the audience pushed past.

Someone was pounding, likely on the blocked doors. The camera whipped into a dizzying spin of the conference room, then stopped at the ceiling.

"Tomas, do we have building video yet?" Marie asked.

"No, Pyre. What I have isn't any help. Off or static. I'm working with them to resolve."

A gunshot cracked, then a moment later, a second sounded. They weren't close enough for a double tap. The crowd mixed angry yells among the panicked screaming.

I jumped when one of the pilots spoke over the intercoms. "We've got turbulence ahead and weather at Smith Reynolds in Winston-Salem, but clearance for approach."

Blood drained from my face and I shivered. I'd yet to experience any major bumps in this little jet. Now it felt tiny.

A young, bearded man leaned over the camera, and the image twisted wildly until he focused on Miranda and two other men in spattered polos running toward the camera. The chairs were wildly strewn across the floor, and he either kept backing up or changing the focus.

The three had almost made it through the chairs when the zombie rematerialized right in front of Miranda. I couldn't tell until Miranda fell back against a toppled chair that her stomach had been stabbed.

The camera man continued to step backward with the angry yells and pounding growing louder as the zombie straddled Miranda. He zoomed in as the zombie sliced open Miranda's blouse. A darkness poured across her skin while the zombie began carving into her chest. The victim appeared to be in shock, until the darkness engulfed her face, but her struggle was weak as she tried to wipe it off.

The view backed out farther, showing the fuzzy frame of the open doors. The camera continued, but the zombie just worked patiently at Miranda's motionless body.

Brave or stupid, he stood outside the doors, filming the scene before authoritative shouts yelled in the silence. The video ended.

"What was the dark stuff crawling up Miranda?" I asked.

"Bugs," answered Tomas.

My earlier interview flashed the rave case across my mind. "Beetles?"

"Could be. I can only get so much resolution at this distance. I guess you'll find out."

There didn't seem any other connection to the rave. I'd have to keep my mind open and not assume.

"Finn, what do you have?" Marie pointed David to the back. "Black coffee."

David flashed me a handsome smile, but I didn't ask for anything. He'd find a way to tie it to my Supernatural fandom.

"The Periapt says Iliodor all over this, but he shies away from zombies."

"He outright speaks against it," I said. Marie's lips tightened, but I continued. "An abomination of our natural gifts," I quoted.

Finn tilted his head in a slight nod, agreeing. "However, he's not against killing someone like Miranda. A powerful state figure who supports the Consociation."

"Maybe not against, but he doesn't commonly get involved in those activities."

"At least not that we've proved." Marie studied me. "What do you have, Kristen?"

David brought Finn a bottle of sweet tea. "I agree with Kristen. Supernatural fans have to stick together."

"Stow it, David. Kristen?"

"I'm not saying it can't be one of Iliodor's people, perhaps gone rogue. I just don't want to build all our assumptions around it. We have a zombie, who had to be created by a witch. We have an amulet that might have belonged to Iliodor at one point. We have a Consociation association with the victims. What we need to focus on is the zombie and the witch who created her."

"Jenny Siregar," said Tomas over the comms. "An Iliodor disciple living in Winston-Salem."

Marie raised an eyebrow at me.

The jet bounced, and David swore. I was pretty sure we, at least Finn, the pilots, and I, would be dying soon.

I had trouble focusing through the flight and didn't relax until we landed on the drenched tarmac in North Carolina. The sky was a dull gray, which felt more like twilight than mid-afternoon. While Finn carried his rifle, I added the ammo bag to my go bag and purse. My knees started to firm up on the walk through a light rain to the small building on the edge of the airport. After getting thoroughly soaked on my previous cases, I wore my rain slicker proudly.

"We'll want to approach carefully," Marie said. "Finn and Kristen, I want you both to pull from Haven when we get to the entrance. Right now, the local FBI have an internal perimeter of fifty feet and an outside cordon of twenty-five with all exit doors locked. We don't know if this zombie is on the loose or even alone."

David snorted. "It's not sticking around. It had its fun, and if Miranda was the target — mission accomplished."

"We have no idea what the mission is." Marie's response was sharp. "It could have ended with Miranda, or it may have other targets. We're not going in unprepared. *If*," she put a heavy emphasis on the word, "this is Iliodor's work, then it could be a trap for any Consociation team who investigates."

"Which would be us," Finn added.

"Yes. Even if it's not Iliodor, whoever created the zombie might have just let it loose, and it could be waiting there."

A pair of FBI agents, two women in the usual dark suits, waited for us inside the small jet terminal. One appeared to know Marie on sight as she smiled, then reverted to a more professional demeanor. The car they'd brought for us was a small tank in size, a black Hummer. I had hoped we'd have a local driving us, but Marie handed her go bag to David while she headed for the driver's door.

There were vests in the vehicle for all of us. I packed the back with Finn, recognizing his need for order, but kept my go bag for the back seat. The huge space in the back worked well for Finn's long legs and left me room for my bag at my feet.

Marie started out of the parking space before I had

myself buckled. "Quick report on your interview this morning, Kristen. We've got a couple minutes."

"Well, it's possible a jinn was involved."

She tilted to view me in the mirror, racing toward the red light at the exit. "Van's theory. What makes you say that?"

"Greg Starr might have been hallucinating, but he saw a gray cloud rise from the bar area with a face in it."

"Might have been hallucinating?" We lurched to a stop at the intersection.

"They took MDMA before going into the rave."

"Hmm. Hug drug." David grinned at me from the front seat, then rattled his mints, offering me one. Especially considering the topic, I shook my head.

"Anything else?" Marie asked. The light changed and the Hummer lurched forward, tires chirping.

"Nothing outstanding. I'll go through Van's map and see who else survived who was in the back bar area. Greg wasn't inclined to mention it, and others might have held back as well."

"Keep at it. Good job."

I kept my eyes down for most of the ride, preferring not to watch as Marie raced us along the airport road then a small highway. When we got downtown, tempered by traffic and lights, I peered out at an eclectic mix of lush green spring growth, old utilitarian block buildings, and modern architecture with patios and glass. The city felt rather relaxed, but it was Sunday.

Lights flashed down the road, and when we came to the intersection blocked off by local police, I almost didn't notice the low building of the conference center compared to the high rise on the left. However, the crossroad declined quickly so that by the next block, the conference center rose to three stories.

Marie pulled up to a frustrated officer trying to wave her away and rolled down her window as he stormed to her door. "Agent Marie Pyre, let me through."

Frustration held his frown in place while he studied our suits. David flashed a handsome smile and a badge, causing the officer to march back to move the barricade. There had to be a dozen local officers with only one FBI agent at the main entrance.

From this side, the conference center was all glass. Marie parked in the middle of the road, as three patrol cars took up one side of the street and an ambulance and two black SUVs waited in front of the building.

"Suit up," she said, turning off the engine.

I had to climb down to get out the door. With rain sprinkling on my hair, I had to strip off my raincoat and suit jacket before grabbing a vest and an FBI jacket — which had no hood. Once again, I'd be a frizzy mess before the day was over. I switched ammo quickly, leaving my usual rounds in my jacket and my back-up piece at my ankle. Shooting people was not my favorite choice, especially when the rounds would leave a toxic residue.

"SSA Pyre?" a short officer asked David. He had a ruddy appearance to his skin and pinched lips for such a round face.

Marie didn't glance up from her gun. "Yes."

His lips twitched, and he moved to her. "We need to get in there and clear the room."

"You've got a count on bodies?" she asked.

"Four." He straightened slightly.

"Has the killer left the area?" She holstered her gun, checking our progress.

"No—"

"Do you have SWAT here?"

His eyes tightened. "They were recalled by the FBI."

"Then we're that team. Liaison with the local FBI." She strode toward the bank of doors. "Move it."

Finn slammed the back of the Hummer closed and kept up with her. David shrugged to the officer, and I scurried behind Finn, trying to keep up.

The inside of the building surprised me. A modern décor, as the glassed front promised, incorporated art exhibits on the walls and had an open feel.

A blond woman with her hair tied back waited for us by the escalators to the lower level. "SSA Pyre?" she asked.

"Agent Carlson?" Marie motioned for the woman to lead the way down the escalator. "What's the situation?"

The woman hurriedly complied and stood sideways on the stairs as we descended. "Doors are closed. Local police pulled one body through the doorway before we arrived, one of the attendees. The room appeared clear, but . . ." She swallowed. "We secured the room as directed, and I have my people outside the service entrances in the maintenance hallways. The same door blocker was used there, and we've left it intact. There's been no sign of any — thing — exiting, but it was a good fifteen minutes before we arrived on site. The police had just reached the room by then."

The beauty of the convention center continued as glass entries let in light from our right and art clustered in displays along the walls between rooms. My eyes flicked from the pieces to the massive hall. The invisible zombie could be anywhere. My pulse rose.

"Witnesses?" Marie asked.

"Sequestered into three rooms upstairs — employees in a fourth." Carlson pointed vaguely back up the escalator.

Ahead were three agents, glancing between us and the doors ahead of them. They appeared alert, possibly nervous. My own chest felt tight.

"We'll have another agent joining us for the interviews."

Carlson led us off the escalator. "They're getting antsy."

"Understood."

"Where do you want us?"

"Here, in the hall. Don't come in, no matter what you hear."

Carlson glanced back. "That's not procedure."

"What are your orders?"

"To follow your directions explicitly and without question."

We'd reached the trio of agents. Marie strode past toward the doors. "Here, no matter what."

She glanced at me, then Finn with the slightest nod. We'd come to the scene, and I hoped we'd be able to stop the zombie here, but I couldn't be sure. A small part of natural preservation also wanted there to be nothing on the other side of the doors, but that would just make our chase take longer. Eventually, we'd have to stand up to the zombie and whoever created it.

Discreetly, I reached out to the Haven realm and dipped two fingers in the white. It felt thin and yielding like cotton candy, and when I tossed it against the doors, the spell lit everyone in white, including one entity waiting for us just on the other side. Dimmer, lying far in the back of the unseen room, I could make out a second living creature.

FOUR

"I've got two life signs," I said.

Finn nodded. "One right in front of us, and the second farther back in the room to the right — prone."

We didn't both have to activate a life detection spell from Haven; any witch in the vicinity would see the white glow.

"Kristen, get ready to bind. Finn, weapon hot. David, open the door, but pull back and keep out of Finn's aim."

As Finn lined up for a shot, I moved just behind his left shoulder and tugged at the crumbling moss green of Dur-Alf for a binding spell.

David sauntered to the door before glancing back at us with a devilish, handsome grin.

The figure close to the door skittered back, midway into the room. They stopped and crouched.

"Wait," I said. Using my left hand, I refreshed the Haven life detection.

I followed Finn as he moved closer and farther left to keep his shot lined up. "Ready?" he asked me.

"Good." My heart pounded in my neck.

At Finn's nod, David swung open the door.

The room appeared much like it had in the video with chairs strewn in disarray and Miranda's body amid them. Light from the windows shadowed everything. The air stunk of viscera. I didn't see any beetles. Other than the faint glow, the zombie, previously Jenny Siregar, was invisible.

I flung my spell at the zombie, whipping around the figure, but it shifted back as I did so. My binding slid off. Already my left hand tugged into Dur-Alf for a second attempt.

Finn fired, and the zombie jolted from the impact. His second shot sent it a step backward, then it dropped flat.

My second bind secured it.

"First down," Finn called out.

David tilted his head around the door and peeked inside. The zombie was still invisible except for the fading glow of Haven. "Take your word for it."

Marie strode past us. "Second entity?"

"Still prone, behind that stage," Finn said.

She stopped just inside the door, and David followed, standing somewhat protectively in front of her. Marie gestured us in. "Kristen, get the amulet. Finn, target the second, but don't fire unless it attacks. We may have a survivor."

Finn led, and I refreshed Haven again, throwing the spell deep into the room. The second form lit brighter. He kept the rifle trained and positioned himself in front of David.

Life detection spells create a fair replica of the physical shape, and the zombie was flat on her back. Haven hadn't completely left her; in fact, it seemed to be more delayed than I might expect. It was one spell I'd used during my time in local enforcement to give me an edge. Once it had led to knowing where to shoot during an incident in a dark alley, and the man had died immediately. Haven had faded much quicker.

"Well . . ." I whispered. Cautious, I readied a hold on Dur-Alf for a shield, but the binding still held the body tight.

Reaching down, I had to guess where the amulet might be. I aimed for the neck, hoping to find the chain.

Bugs squirmed under my fingers, and I yipped, pulling back. My face warmed, and I grimaced as I dug through them for the chain.

"What?" Marie asked.

"Bugs." I felt the chain, ignored what crawled between my fingers, and found the amulet.

Immediately, the zombie and bugs were visible. She had multiple holes in her chest, and the bugs flowed in and out of them. My jaw tightened.

My own hand, arm, and body disappeared. I yanked the long chain over her head and hair, grimacing and shaking my invisible hand as the unseen bugs crawled toward my sleeves. Dancing slightly, I tossed the amulet between me and the others, then vigorously shook the bugs off.

"Put it in your pocket," Marie said. "Skin contact activates it, but supposedly users can control their invisibility."

Disdainfully, between the bugs and stench, I retrieved the amulet, jiggling off a lone bug. It could have been a beetle but appeared more like a roach.

"Careful with that blade. It has runes on it." Marie kept her eyes on the stage and gestured toward an engraved knife with an eight-inch blade. The silver metal appeared seamless through the hilt. "David, recover that."

I slid the amulet in my pocket gingerly and focused on

the figure lying behind the stage. Even with the gray skies outside, the window was bright, interfering with a clear view of the Haven glow on the body.

As David stepped forward to pick up and inspect the blade, I formed a wide shield between us and the stage. Spread out, it would be thinner and less resistant. A stronger witch might have been able to do more, but I knew my limits.

Waiting until David had secured the blade, Marie called out. "FBI, identify yourself."

The shape didn't move. Marie moved forward with the rest of us stepping up to maintain our group. "FBI. Are you injured?"

A pane in the high bank of windows shattered. My shield flickered as a bullet passed through and thudded into a wall behind Marie's head. I pulled on Dur-Alf for a second shield as another bullet made it through my first.

The sharp scent of vinegar rose above the stench in the room. I placed my second shield in front of Marie even as she and David spread away from us. A bullet hit the thicker consistency and slid to the side before dropping to the floor near her.

Finn had relaxed his hold on his rifle and pulled a shield to place close to the broken window.

A second pane shattered, seemingly tracking Marie's movements. I condensed the first to protect her. "They're shooting at Marie!" I yelled. Still holding two shields, I scraped a third off of Dur-Alf.

I barely noticed when the fading Haven glow behind us shifted.

Finn had seen it as well. "We've got movement." He would have to release his shields to fire.

A bullet and then another ricocheted off Finn's shield

close to the window. They stunk of vinegar, reminding me of our own ammo.

From behind the stage rose a lich. No more than bones encased in tattered black clothes, it floated up with an ornate staff held impossibly in a skeletal hand. A tarnished helmet had spikes like a crown perched on its gray skull. Once a witch, a lich could pull at the realms, and this one touched Haven with bony fingers.

It threw a ball of fire and heat toward Marie, the only damaging spell we knew could be drawn from Haven. Flames whipped across my multiple shields and darted across the floor and walls, scorching them.

A second spell followed the first as the lich floated higher in front of the windows. An inferno erupted across my shields, but they held. Marie stepped back from the heat.

I chanced a fourth spell, holding one with my left hand and digging in again for a binding spell. The effort had me sweating, and my knees might have given out if my heart weren't pounding so hard.

Marie's tail whipped out, weaving among our shields and the dwindling flames.

I slung my binding spell, but the lich slid away at the touch of it.

David stepped in front of Finn, his gun drawn, and fired. A number of windows exploded behind the lich. I swore ratty cloth flicked at its legs.

The cryptid flew backward, away from David and the shots. Ragged robes fluttered with its increasing speed. The screech it let out echoed above the crack of David's weapon.

The lich pulled from Haven again and turned invisible.

David emptied his magazine where the cryptid had last been.

I kept the shields up protecting Marie and dipped two fingers into Haven, creating another life detection spell.

The lich was nowhere in the room. "It's gone."

Marie headed for the exit. "Move it."

I backed out slowly, holding the shields in case the sniper decided I was worth it. Bugs squirmed across the zombie. This had been a trap aimed at Marie. Iliodor had planned a similar plot before to assassinate top Consociation officials and succeeded. He hadn't used a zombie or anything from Tarus, though.

"Finn, double time. I don't want to lose the track."

"Got it, Pyre."

My skin crawled as I remembered him using Ya Keya to track in Atlanta. It was too dangerous.

I sagged as I released my shields and turned to search for the others. Marie was already at the escalator with David close behind. Finn had stowed his weapon in the holster on his back and had covered half the distance between me and the others.

"Shit." I scrambled into a run, drawing worried glances from the FBI guarding the exit doors from which our team was running away at full speed. "It's okay, stay put." None of them seemed calmed by my instruction.

Marie and David climbed the upward escalator, racing ahead of me. "Did you see the marks carved on Miranda's chest? Iliodor's rune." She spoke in the comms, but I didn't know if she expected a response.

David answered. "Yeah, I saw that."

A lot of evidence pointed toward Iliodor. The amulet, the rune on the victim's chest, and Jenny Siregar, the acolyte turned zombie. This had been about Marie, and she had a vengeance for Iliodor. Beyond his obvious interference with Consociation aims, I didn't know if she had another reason for her grudge. The leads could be manipulated, just to point her in a certain direction or with hope she became sloppy in her pursuit.

David and Marie disappeared at the top of the escalator as Finn reached it and started climbing.

Marie spoke over the comms. "Tomas, contact Carlson and let her know to hold tight. Clear the cleanup team to retrieve the bodies and get them back to Herta. Total of four. Coordinate them with Carlson. Let me know when Leah's on site." The background noise turned louder with the sounds of traffic. "Finn, front passenger. Kristen, move it."

My legs ached as I ran up the escalator stairs. When I burst out of the doors, heads turned to watch me sprint to the Hummer, already running. The scent of rain accompanied a drizzle.

I barcly had the door closed when Marie gunned it down the street toward the barricade at the next corner. She leaned on the horn as I scrambled for my seat buckle. The wipers weren't even on, leaving a watery view ahead.

Finn's rifle case rested between me and David. The scent of burnt plastic hung in the vehicle. How much heat had Marie endured? Her FBI jacket appeared puckered at the shoulder.

"Put that away," she said to Finn. "You can call in the Kuru later."

"Too late," he said. "Done."

"Focus."

The gun case slid into me as she nearly clipped the agent pulling aside the barricade before she turned onto the cross street.

"Wrong way. One way!" Finn's usual calm tone rose, alerting me to our situation.

I made the mistake of glancing up and peering out the front window. A tiny blue coupe blasted its horn as it screeched to a stop, but she just swerved left of them to the middle of the three lanes. Indeed, the arrows all pointed at us. The convention center stretched down the entire block along our right side. Two more vehicles were heading down the street toward us.

My eyes locked open as a box truck tilted forward in our lane and added its horn to the symphony. The last vehicle, a Volkswagen bug with peeling pink paint, continued behind the blue coupe, forcing Marie to swerve further to the left. As soon as she passed the truck, we veered back to the right.

At the intersection ahead, cars waited, filling all three lanes. I couldn't see the lights because they weren't aimed for a direction we shouldn't be going. Marie gunned it, slamming me back, but I didn't release my death grip on the gun case and couldn't close my eyes. A pickup started to turn onto our street and stopped halfway. She didn't start to slow for the corner until I could see the angry faces of the drivers on the opposite side.

As we screeched around the corner, I finally took a breath. Finn began tugging at Ya Keya and Haven. My hand still gripping the gun case quivered. We were, at least, on a two way street.

David rattled his mints, offering me them to me. When I shivered a shake of my head, he leaned toward the front. "The blade has arcane runes designed to 'expel' from the Earth realm. Devastating on Merfolk, dwarves, or dragon-shifters such as yourself. Might do something nasty to good people such as myself, as well."

"Send pictures to Tomas." Marie slowed, peering at Finn and not watching the street at all. Glass crunched under the tires.

"They were after you, Pyre." David spoke as he carefully pulled the blade from his jacket.

"I know. Now we're after them. Stow it."

My heart raced, and I focused on my bag at my feet. David motioned for me to hold the blade still as he placed it on the seat between us and dug out his phone.

Grateful for something to stare at besides Marie not watching the road, I spoke quietly, mainly to myself. "How do we not die?" I should be worried about Finn, manipulating Ya Keya to search for the lich.

David answered, absently snapping pictures of the knife. "Dragon-shifters have levels of vision, taste, and hearing to match their dragon brains. Their replication of human sensory organs is not quite legit." He grinned and took a picture of my expression. "Cheating if you ask me."

"Stow it, David."

He mocked an abashed grimace and delicately picked up the knife. Despite his explanation, I wouldn't be too much more assured that she wasn't going to kill me and Finn in a fiery accident someday.

"Got it." Finn gestured across the front of the Hummer, ahead and to Marie's left.

Tires squealed, and I closed my eyes.

S itting with my eyes closed behind Marie as we swerved through traffic with horns blazing didn't make me any less sure of our impending deaths.

I opened my eyes when she slammed us to a stop, cursed, and pumped the horn as she crossed a red light. The daylight dimmed, racing between tall buildings under gray skies.

Turning, I spoke quietly to David. "The ammo they used, it had a vinegar scent. I've noticed it before. It may be the same ammo our team uses." Deadly to most, it might be damaging to a dragon-shifter depending upon center mass hit.

"That would be a twist," he said.

"Another weight in Iliodor's favor." Marie spoke alongside Finn's newest report on a sighting of the lich's trail. "I don't even think he cared about Miranda; this was a trap designed for me."

"I agree with the ambush part. We were drawn here. A public assassination of a Consociation — associate. The news would pop up quickly on Tomas's radar, and we'd be on our way. The sniper could have taken out any of us when we walked through the door. They didn't try until they had a clear shot of you. The lich focused everything on you."

"But you still won't buy in on Iliodor." Her tone edged on annoyance.

"Not fully. Mainly because of the zombie. I do believe someone has gone through the effort to make sure we believe it *is* Iliodor, though."

We didn't need to argue about this. Our path wove down through a road between two brick mills or factories that appeared abandoned. I changed the subject. "I think David hit the lich. Will the bullet kill it, eventually?"

David shook his head. "Not much to hit. Bones held up by Earth magic. Killing it would require a lucky shot, or a very close target. Probably came near enough to kick in self-preservation." He unbuckled his seatbelt. "Reminds me, I need more ammo. I'm on my backup magazine."

Finn's shot at the demon and my shot at the opening to Tarus had both been into something less than corporeal, and they'd worked. David might be wrong.

He was leaning over the back when Finn pointed at a scorched hole in the side of an abandoned building. Marie slammed on the brakes, sending David ass first to the front, then she swerved left toward the opening.

"In there?" she asked.

Finn pushed David back toward me. "Yes."

Folded nearly in half, David grinned. "Stick shift, I'm guessing.'"

Marie turned off the Hummer as she opened the door. "Move it."

The rain had turned to mist, but the clouds above did not appear finished. They were darker, or it was later than

I thought. The street had little traffic on a Sunday afternoon.

When we approached the opening, I had two shields up. I was tired, so they'd be weak. Finn covered with his rifle.

David put his hand in front of Marie, stopping her from leading. "Beauty before — um, let me go first."

She gave him a sharp glare. Bricks lay strewn around the opening and inside in the darkness as far as I could see. We stepped through slowly, David leading.

The room had dingy brown walls with holes in the drywall as if someone had ripped out piping or conduit. Dust swirled from the slight breeze.

I adjusted the two shields to overlap as David stepped inside. Marie followed, obviously impatient as she peered around him. There was only blackness ahead.

When Finn stepped in beside me, I realized I'd left my flashlight in my go bag. What was the point of packing it if I forgot it? I'd gotten lax. We walked across a large room with walls torn apart from scavenging. Slightly to the right stood a door with motionless shadows beyond, and I adjusted my shield between the opening and David.

On the other side of the doorway, the long hall ahead was lit with red. A raging fireball raced along the narrow confines and burst into our room, splashing against my shields. David nearly stepped into the flames to fire around my shields. He couldn't see them, but the fire outlined them.

Finn's rifle shot at my right told me he'd done the same. Marie's impossibly long tail stretched over my shields and darted down the hall. The walls smoked, and embers glowed in areas. Belatedly, I snipped at Haven and lit the shape of the lich with the detection.

"It's moving to the right," I yelled.

Marie's tail whipped back, startling me so that when she raced forward, I barely kept my shields ahead of her. Scurrying behind David, I left Finn behind us. The stench of burnt dust and drywall clung in the air.

The lich paused and began to separate into two glowing white forms. "There's something else now. Two."

Marie reached the end of the hall, and the best I could do was angle the shields as fire blasted into them. Flames licked down onto her. My hair would have gone up. Straining, I pulled a third shield and threw it to overlap her head before the second fireball reached her. David stood beside her firing as flames singed his suit sleeve to sparks.

The second shape charged as if entering the adjacent room. I barely realized what it was doing when a pure white light hit my shields. It had no heat, but the brilliance of Haven's light blinded me.

Blinking, I held the shields, hoping Marie did not move out of their protection. The wall beside me crashed, and a sheet of drywall slapped against me, knocking me to the far side. Panic tightened my chest. The scent of musk and fur hung in the air. I couldn't guess where to defend myself, but I dragged up a fourth shield, leaving three on Marie and David.

Finn screamed.

I dropped the fourth shield and kept blinking as I pushed aside the broken drywall. The world was a gray mire with moving shadows. Something strong slapped the board as I moved it. I glimpsed the motion. It snorted, and I imagined a werewolf there. Reaching for a binding spell, no matter how futile it may be in my present situation, I hoped to catch the creature in front of me. At least, it would abandon its attack on Finn.

What could have been Marie's tail rasped against my FBI jacket and shot past me. I hoped it was her.

A beastly howl screamed nearly in my face. Unable to blink past the grayness and spots, I stumbled back. A gunshot cracked from behind me.

I froze, then heard a heavy body slam onto the ground. Marie's tail slid past me, returning to her. My peripheral vision caught a hoof or paw kick out near my feet.

I stumbled back another step, then called out. "Finn?"

"Shit . . ." he responded in a pained voice.

Unsure, I stepped toward his voice, catching hints of the wall at the edge of my vision. I caught the shape of a fallen body, but hairy rather than clothed in pants. Grimacing, I tried to step over it and nearly tripped when I kicked into what might have been a leg. Shuffling my feet, I made my way past.

"Pyre," David called out. "We can't follow. Don't chase it alone. You're the only one who wouldn't be affected by the light. They might know that and be trying to separate us."

Her growl came over the comms.

"Finn? I can't see." I thought he might be close, from his earlier outburst.

"I've got pressure on it." His voice was strained, but it gave me a sense of where he was.

My toe tapped the bottom of his shoe, and I felt the wall, preparing to slide down.

"Night storms," Marie's voice sounded behind me before she brushed past. "Tomas, we've lost the lich. Track whatever you can to get us a location. We need emergency medical for Finn. Send local FBI to cordon off the opening; they are not to enter. David, text the Kuru — yes, I know they don't like you." She smelled singed.

Shifting my head, I could catch vague glimpses of what I believed was Marie crouched in front of me. Finn groaned as she moved. Turning helped me gather the shape of the creature she'd killed. An overly long arm rested over its middle section, and the distinct shape of a horn rested on what remained of the opposite wall. "Is that a minotaur?" A huge hole had been torn in the drywall. It had come straight through into Finn.

"Yep." I jumped when David spoke beside me. "Still blind?" he asked.

Flashes of light sparked in the darkness of my vision, but I was learning to use my peripheral vision, sweeping past areas I wanted to see. Haven's light spell had made me useless. "Is Finn okay?"

"He's unconscious. The horn missed his femoral artery. Might have broken his femur from the position of his leg. I've got the wound compressed with my belt. Tomas, ETA on medical?"

"Two and half minutes, Pyre."

She stood, and I could recognize the movement. My sight was better.

"You aren't drawing your weapon," Marie said in a straightforward tone, without any hint of reproach.

"I — well, I'm holding spells or preparing them." I'd been maintaining three shields over her which would have been more difficult with a weapon in my hand.

"Humans do use their hands for this. It makes sense."

Did it? My whole career I'd hid my magic, and now I could utilize it fairly freely with the Consociation's blessing. Before, my gun had been my weapon. I'd always wished I could use magic instead.

"David, can you see again?" Marie asked.

"Rebooted and ready to go, Pyre."

"Kristen, wait here with Finn, collect his weapon, and head back with him. David, with me."

"Are you going to track the lich?"

"We'll try, though it's getting dark. Tomas, you're wired into local social media and emergency bands?"

He swore. "Of course."

"Move it." Her steps led away, and David passed me.

I knelt, touching Finn's shoe lightly, then shuffled forward, careful not to touch his leg. His rifle was tucked by his side, and his hand rested limply over it. I picked up his hand and held it.

The Hummer started outside and chirped away.

The hall, or what was left of it, had only the dim light from the opening in the adjacent room. It didn't help. Now that the sharp scent of Marie's toasted jacket was gone, I caught the pungent funk of the dead minotaur beside me.

"Well, this isn't going well, is it?" I whispered quietly, then cringed, remembering the comms.

Gary, Finn's husband, would be horrified to find out about the attack. We couldn't tell him details, but the damage alone would be enough. The biggest issue they had seemed to be the risks Finn took in his job.

It could have been me who'd been attacked. My daughter Jade had no idea of what I dealt with, but she'd had her vision of me trapped in Tarus. That haunted her enough.

A siren peeped in the streets outside, then let out a longer wail before going silent. Tires crunched outside, then doors clanged shut. I could make out the opening as two figures arrived.

"Kristen Winters? Finn Billings?" a woman asked.

"Yes."

I pushed back from Finn, and the soles of my shoes pushed against the dead minotaur, causing me to grimace. She squeezed in, dropping a case beside her. Lights flashed, and I was grateful that I could see him better. His pants were wet with blood on the left leg, and Marie had tied her belt above his knee.

"Unresponsive, but he's good for transport. Get the gurney."

The other shape had disappeared back out the ragged hole the lich had made. Marie and David now chased it alone. Whoever was after Marie could be trying to drain off her support. Her obsession with Iliodor didn't help matters. She could have waited until we had Finn somewhere safe, then we all could have gone after the lich. Her decisions might be colored by her emotions.

"Are you accompanying him?" the woman asked.

"Yes." I wanted to be there when Finn woke up.

CHAPTER
SIX

The emergency vehicle bounced as it rambled down another rural back road northwest of Winston-Salem. Finn's leg had been bandaged up, an IV connected to a bag hanging above him, and straps kept him secured to the gurney. After seeing David convalescing in our employee lounge, I expected that we wouldn't be heading to a hospital, but we'd been on the road for ten minutes, and we were passing farms.

David and Marie were circling the north area of the city where the lich had escaped. She wasn't tolerating his banter well. Tomas hadn't gotten a hint of any leads, and considering the lich's ability to use Haven's invisibility spell, I doubted they would find any trail.

If the deaths at the convention center were an attempt to ambush Marie, we were dealing with somebody invested in eliminating her. They'd had a blade and ammunition sufficient to do the job. The focus on her had been too obvious to ignore. A powerful witch or arcane user could both zombify Jennifer Siregar and summon a lich. It didn't have to be Iliodor. "Marie, David, are they okay?" Finn's voice was scratchy, dry.

I smiled at hearing his voice, weak but alert. "They're uninjured, searching."

The passenger in the front of the truck slid out of her seat, and I moved farther toward the back to give her room. She was about my age, but more athletically built with short black hair. She wore an EMT uniform with a Winston-Salem insignia. "How are you feeling?" she asked Finn as she began checking vitals. "Dizzy, nausea, headache?"

I took a deep, calm breath, the first since we'd trundled Finn out of the building. My eyes were restored, but I had the edge of headache. I didn't get the migraines my daughter did. Those were more from her sensitivity to realms than any normal human condition. I tried not to grab onto anything delicate as we turned a corner.

In a few seconds we slowed, and I peered out the windshield at another country road with a couple business and parking lots before it turned to woods leading up a hill. To the right was a propane tank, pallets, and an old storage barn with bags of mulch and such. We turned left.

"Where are we?" Checking the back window, I answered my own question as the driver backed up to an animal hospital. "Well, that makes sense."

"What?" asked Marie over the comms. "Are you at the veterinary hospital yet? How's Finn?"

"He's not feline well."

"Of course he's not. Let me know what they say."

David chuckled in the background for my benefit.

I stood around awkwardly as they maneuvered Finn inside. His smiles were weak, but he tried to make me more comfortable about the situation, so I acted as if this were a perfectly normal place to take him. At least it wasn't raining, though the clouds still hung dark over us.

The side door let us into a tight hall with bathrooms ahead of us and a lobby to the left at the front of the building. An older man with a white beard and graying temples led us through a door to the right where the hall continued with four doors and a window.

A vet's hardly seemed the appropriate place. The surprise came when they set him up in a well-equipped, windowless back room with a full hospital bed. There was a sink and cabinets and even a pair of end tables to one side near a comfortable chair. Exhausted from the use of so much magic, my eyes flicked at it longingly.

My go bag was with Marie and David, but I couldn't do anything about it. I'd likely be here for a while. The bearded man had disappeared, though he might be the vet. There had to be a Consociation doctor on the way.

The two EMTs, if they were such, set Finn up in the bed, hung his IV, and closed the door behind them, leaving us alone.

"Painful?" I asked him.

"Dull." He nudged a chin toward the IV bag. "Doping me up with something."

"Want me to see if I can find you something to drink?" I swallowed, trying not to be selfish.

The door opened and a small man in a white lab coat came in, eyes focused on the wall straight ahead. As he closed it behind him, the illusion puckered between his neck and arm.

"Hi, are you here to work on Finn?" I wouldn't know who should be coming to help, but I guessed this was a dwarf healer.

"Yes." If I'd thought Tomas's voice was high pitched, the dwarf sounded like an animated chipmunk.

The illusion distorted as the dwarf jumped up to the bed, and the knees bent sideways in an unsettling manner. I suddenly was very grateful for Udy.

Almost brusquely, distorting hands removed the bandages from Finn's bare leg. Angry red flesh puckered out of his brown skin. Two inches wide at least, the laceration began leaking bright blood immediately.

Finn's slacks had been cut off mid thigh, and he patted at the tattered edge of them. "How's it look?" His speech had gotten thicker.

"Lovely. They told me minotaur horn. Are you sure?" The head swiveled to stare at the wall above my head. The shoulders never flinched from the movement.

Between the voice and the disquieting illusion, I shivered. "Yes. Minotaur."

"Are you well, dear? You look pale."

I forced a smile. "I'm fine. Will he be okay?"

"Fit as a violin. It'll take time. He won't be walking. I can only do so much with bone. It's like a stein freshly glued back together. His flesh will take me a couple hours."

Finn lifted his head. "Gary."

The head spun back, staring forward and nowhere near Finn's face. "No, Dowlin. Name's Dowlin, dear. Lie back."

Marie said something under her breath, further muffled by the comms before she spoke clearly. "Tell Finn we'll let Gary know and get him out here tomorrow morning. It's going to be the three of us on this case now. I hate losing Finn."

"What about Leah, Pyre?" asked Tomas.

"We'll have her help with interviews; that will be something, and more than we can handle from the volume of it."

I found my lips tightened, and loosened them to

acknowledge and relay the information to Finn about his husband. Marie certainly seemed less concerned about Finn than she was about the lich. We did have to stop it and whoever had summoned it. We'd need Tomas and the Consociation's eyes and ears to find it, though. Her demeanor probably shouldn't have bothered me, but it did.

Finn wasn't very responsive, but he appeared relieved about Gary waiting until morning. "Be better then." His voice was slow and his tongue thick. I had to hope he'd sleep while the dwarf worked. He reached out his hand, searching for mine. "Lich?" he asked.

I held his hand. "David and Marie are searching," I said.

"Go." He barely whispered.

Dowlin let out a loud click. "Minotaurs and lichs. You humans are depraved. You know what a lich is?"

I repeated the rote information all witches were taught as a warning. "A witch who sacrifices themselves as they enter Tarus." It had been more common ages ago when magic was new to witches and some witches considered it a concept of immortality, like vampires.

"Normal folk don't do that. Abominations." Her squeaky voice peaked at the latter word. I had thought Dowlin one of the more pleasant dwarves I'd met, but my experience was limited, and she'd become somewhat callous on this topic.

"It is unknown for a witch to do that in today's times." My response held a sharper tone than I intended.

"And yet, humans are still meddling, or there wouldn't be a lich in this realm. Depraved. Even the merfolk have enough sense not to dabble with dangerous realms. If Dur-Alf were adjacent to Tarus or Ya Keya, you wouldn't see us touching those realms. You've always been a strange, dangerous lot."

Marie sighed in the comms. "Let it be, Kristen. It's not an argument you can win. Go grab something to eat. I'm heading back to the scene with David, and we'll start interviews with Leah's help. You'll be with Finn until we can transport him in a couple hours."

Tomas piped up. "Leah's on site. No comms, but she's got her phone."

Dowlin's illusion didn't move from its strange perch atop the bed. Finn's eyelids were drooping. There wasn't anything I could do, and he seemed out of danger. The wound was still an angry red, but the bleeding had stopped.

I squeezed Finn's hand. "I'm going to get something to eat. I'll be right back." The rural setting might offer less than I expected.

"Pizza," he said.

"He *will* be hungry, dear. You've got time. I'll be here." Gratefully, the dwarf's illusionary head didn't swivel toward me. Despite considering us depraved humans, she was helping Finn and not nearly as brusquely as Herta would have.

"Thank you." I headed for the door, pulling out my phone. "When you said he wouldn't be walking — you meant for a couple days, right?"

"Yes, dear. I'll work on him for about four days to make sure nothing clots or such, then he'll be on crutches."

Before I opened the door, Marie entered the conference center, speaking to Agent Carlson. The woman spoke quietly, but I could make out part of it.

". . . sequestered in a room on the top floor with an officer from the local Winston-Salem police. I just found out they let the employees go home."

"Dancing monkeys." Marie normally didn't lose her

calm demeanor very often, but she raised her voice. "Get them back here."

David was calmer. "Pyre, Tomas can track them. If one of them is a problem, we'll know it when they bolt. Might work out for the best."

"Okay." Her tone was still aggressive. "Where's Leah?" Her comms cut off at the end, and her words came through David's before he too, turned off his comms.

I paused with my hand on the knob before I sagged and trudged into the short but well-lit hall and exited the door at the end, finding the bathrooms there with a weak smile. It had gotten dark outside. Streetlights lit the empty parking lot. The rest of the building appeared dark, and I had to flick on the bathroom light when I entered. Marie had mentioned transporting Finn, but to where?

When I exited, a male's voice called from the dim lobby. "How's it going?"

I strode to the corner, unsure how much I should be wandering around. The white bearded man sat behind the counter with an open book under a small light. Stepping forward, I smiled. "Well, they're working on him."

He placed a receipt into his book and stood. "Good. Been a while since we've needed the room. I'm Dr. Kines." Approaching, he offered his hand.

"Agent Kristen Winters." As I shook his hand, a hint of Haven glowed around him. My grandmother could heal with Haven, but I'd never gotten very far with it. Perhaps the vet used it in his practice.

His white bushy eyebrows rose. "Rough day?"

He likely saw remnants of Dur-Alf around me. I couldn't tell him much, and he hadn't really probed too deep. "Yeah. Looking for someplace to get food." I peered out the front windows into the darkness where there was no sign of anything. "Pizza, if possible."

Dr. Kines jerked a thumb over his shoulder. "I've got quinoa and kale, if you want me to heat it up."

Gary would like Dr. Kines, if we were still here when he got to town. I offered an apologetic grin. "Is there someplace that delivers pizza, maybe?"

He shrugged. "Domino's. A minute's walk." He gestured toward the front and down the right.

I studied the dark windows, leaning to get more of a view. One building had a dim light, but it appeared closed. "A minute?"

I left the building with Dr. Kines' simple directions, and only as the wind chilled my cheeks did I realize I still wore my vest. An hour later, after I'd appreciated the warmth the vest and jacket provided, I returned with two pizzas, minus a couple of slices, and two bottles of water. The kindly witch with a beard had a different sense of a quick walk than I did.

He was still reading and had no interest in the pizza.

Dowlin's illusion remained in the same position, but the head swiveled completely around when I entered. The Consociation should have sent someone to help with the illusion. Finn was asleep, David and Marie had turned off their comms when they'd started interviews, and I couldn't be much help to anyone.

"Pizza?" I asked.

"Ugh. You know they use body fluids to make that, don't you?" Dowlin's head turned forward again. "Body parts too, I've heard."

Her opinion wasn't going to stop me. "Yeah. I'll take that as a no." Placing the pizza on one of the little tables, I sunk into the chair with a grateful moan. It was past 9:00 p.m., and I was hungry.

"You and the Kuru." Dowlin pronounced their name differently than the team did.

I perked up at the mention, but grabbed a slice. "What about them?"

"Carnivores. Nipping after anything they can sneak up on."

My eyebrows raised. "What do they look like?"

"Oh, dear, we don't talk about that, do we?" She sounded joyful, though with her chipmunk voice, everything had sounded almost happy.

My comms clicked as I took a bite. Marie's voice sounded over them. "How soon can we move Finn?"

I swallowed quickly, nearly choking. "Dowlin, when can Finn be moved?" The wound had been healed from an angry red to a pale pink ripple in Finn's skin.

"Give me another thirty minutes, dear. I can check on him regularly after we give him a short rest."

"Got it." Marie clicked her comms off again.

I never got to ask *where* we'd be transporting Finn.

CHAPTER

SEVEN

When the transport company came to fetch Finn, they brought a wheelchair for him. A young woman named Latoya came to the veterinarian's hospital, but she didn't ask any questions as we bundled Finn into the chair with Dowlin's hands regularly warping whenever she reached for anything. I cheated, using a lifting spell from Mer to help, though even with it, I wouldn't have been able to lift Finn myself. Some witches could lift more than their own weight; I wasn't one.

While I held the door open, Finn woke as she wheeled him out. "Hey." His voice was still thick. He poked at the inflatable cast around his leg, which the woman had brought. "Cool."

"How do you feel?"

"Drugged." He swayed slightly as she turned him. "David? Marie?"

"At the scene — the first one."

The van had a lift, and she locked him onto it. He studied the two boxes of pizza in my hands. "Are those for me?"

"Well . . ."

The lift began to rise, and Finn's eyebrows furrowed. "What?"

"Never mind, it's too cheesy."

Finn laughed, but he *was* drugged.

Dowlin's head swiveled, peering at each of us.

Fifteen minutes later we pulled up to a hotel across from a Wendy's. The main section had seven floors, but it wasn't very big. The driver handed me four hotel room cards. "103 and 105. Ground floor." I thought she was going to send us in alone, but she wheeled Finn, and I scurried ahead to open the door. Dowlin followed slowly behind us, and luckily we barely caught a glance from the man at the front desk.

When we got to the first room, I opened it for Finn and Latoya, who pushed his wheelchair, while Dowlin waited at the other. I had mistakenly assumed one room would be mine. When the dwarf entered, she pointed at the door that adjoined the two rooms. "Open that, both sides." As I opened her side, the illusion dropped away and she sighed. "Gadz that's exhausting. Thank you, dear."

Dowlin had a youthful, if furry, face. She might have been three feet tall with the same brown skin and purple eyes Herta had, though Dowlin wore no glasses. Her black hair had been braided into a conical bun on her head.

"You're welcome." I tried not to stare.

She pointed to the locked door of the other room. "You'll need to go around to let me in."

I flushed and hurried back into the corridor. As I opened Finn's door, my comms crackled.

"Kristen, hitch a ride with the transport and get back here. We're swamped in interviews."

"Okay. Will do."

The woman had Finn standing on one leg and pivoting

to sit on the bed. I threw a lifting spell to steady him, and he chuckled and sat down. Dowlin tapped on the adjoining door.

"Marie wants me back at the scene. Are you going to be okay?" I dropped pizza boxes by the television, unlocked the door to Dowlin's room, and tried to straighten my frizz — unsuccessfully.

"Fine. I'm hungry."

I moved the pizza to the bed. "Latoya, can you drop me off?"

She nodded silently, easing Finn back onto his pillows. He grimaced but appeared relaxed otherwise.

Dowlin stared up at me. "That was a joke. Cheesy."

I blushed. "Sorry. It wasn't fair to poke fun at a man with a broken leg — it's not humerus."

Finn chuckled and pointed toward the door. "Get out."

The rain had stopped by the time Latoya dropped me at the convention center. The puddled street had been reopened, and Marie's Hummer and two black SUVs were parked in the drop off area. There was no sign of local police. A young FBI agent waited at the entrance and raised his hand until I showed him my badge. I had assumed the jacket and vest would have been enough to get me in. A car's tires sluiced over the wet road behind me while he opened the doors.

As I entered the expansive lobby, I spoke into my comms. "I'm on site." The building appeared empty. The Kuru had likely cleared the room downstairs, and the Consociation would have picked up the victim's corpses. Tomas would have let us know if any word of the lich had surfaced. We were down to interviews at this point. I probably had emails to check. I'd grown curious to meet Leah as well.

"Downstairs," was all Marie said.

Lips pinching together, I strode for the escalator and pulled out my phone. I had just scrolled the list of emails when Marie burst out of a conference room, glanced at me, and marched to the next room to rap on the door. I hurried down the steps of the escalator.

"We've got eight left. They're getting irate." She motioned to a cluster of FBI agents talking in the hall. "Hey," she yelled down to them.

David stepped out of the room she'd rapped on. He'd donned his suit again, without the vest, and beamed handsomely as he approached. "Glad you could join the fun. How's Finn?"

"Well, groggy, but the wound is healed. His leg was broken."

A middle-aged agent jogged toward us. Marie pointed to one of the conference rooms. "Kristen, set up in there. Tomas hasn't flagged anyone as a priority in our databases. David, have you gotten anything we should focus on? I'm not getting anything new. Same variations of what we've seen."

He shook his head. "Same old." A sly grin formed at the edge of his mouth. "I did get one number. Will we be spending the night?"

She ignored David and spoke to the agent as he arrived. "This is SA Kristen Winters. Get her set up in that room for interviews. We should be done in less than an hour with four of us."

The man had a graying mustache, and it twitched before he cleared his throat. "We don't have another recorder. We gave our last to your other agent." He motioned down the hall, where I imagined Leah was interviewing a witness.

Marie raised a hand in acquiescence, then turned to

me. "Use your phone to record; otherwise, Tomas can pull it off the comms."

"I can record on my phone." It had been fully charged when I got off the plane.

She nodded to the agent. "Please get her one of the witnesses."

As he moved out of range, I asked, "Any word on the lich?"

"I wouldn't be here. Tomas is staying at the office tonight and monitoring. If we don't hear anything by the time we're done, we'll check Jenny Siregar's apartment and see what we can find out. What do you have, Kristen?"

I blinked and stifled a shrug. "I was with Finn."

"You've been thinking, beyond Iliodor." Marie waited.

"The sniper. A witch or an arcane user, a very skilled one, could create a zombie and even summon a lich, but neither of them could compel a sniper. They'd have to hire him. A demon or jinn could compel, but I'm not sure they could create a zombie, and they can't summon." The pieces floated in my mind like character cards being played. "We are certainly looking for at least a witch or arcane user, but we shouldn't dismiss how the sniper came into the game."

My phone rang in my hand. Heat warmed my cheeks, and I hastily hung up on Jade. I could text her when Marie wasn't standing there. My pulse had already risen just detailing my concern. I hadn't even mentioned the locked doors. Who had done that?

Marie nodded. "That doesn't preclude Iliodor."

"It doesn't, but you've heard my argument against his involvement."

"Good. Keep at it." She gestured toward the agent with the gray mustache and the angry man in a white shirt carrying his suit jacket. "Release them unless there's something particular I need to hear."

When I opened the door for the scowling witness, I pasted a smile on my face and tried not to think about how late it was. I was drained. "Sorry for the delay. I'm Special Agent Winters. Please come in."

"Do you have any idea how long I've sat in that room? The crappy deli food didn't help." The man's thin face might have been handsome without the snarl. He didn't have Tomas's green eyes, but the thin build and shorter height offered some similarities. "They took our phones."

"You'll get them back." I motioned him to one of the chairs in the back row.

"When?"

I had no idea, but my comms were active, so I waited to respond as I pulled aside a chair for myself, facing him. It took a moment for Tomas to reply, "They're cleaned. The FBI have them along with a waiver they'll have to sign at release."

"As soon as we're done here." I pulled out my phone, texting Jade I was still working and would call if it wasn't too late. The time difference left some hope.

"Hurry up, then." He took his seat after throwing his jacket over the back of a nearby chair.

"I'll be recording this interview for our notes." I tapped off my comms and set the phone to record, placing it on a chair next to us. "What is your name?"

"Derrick Matheson."

"Where were you seated?"

"In the audience, with everyone else." His tone bristled my frustration.

I spoke slowly, dragging out my words. "This interview will take longer if you generalize your statements. I would rather we move quickly, but we can only do that if you answer the questions in detail. Otherwise, I'll have to repeat my questions. Where, in the audience, were you seated?"

His hands clenched, then he blew audibly through his nose. "Fifth row on the right side, about the third chair from the outside aisle. Next to Gloria Gaines; we both work at the same company."

"Excellent. Did you notice anything unusual before the first attack?"

"Other than Miranda Powell having three security guards, nothing." His lips moved as if he might say more, but remained silent.

I chalked it up to holding back a snide remark and moved on. "Describe what you saw of the first attack."

His pale face blanched whiter. "A crapload of blood. I'm glad we weren't in those front rows."

"Did you see the attacker?"

"A crazy, naked chick with black hair." His scowl had left, but I found the man less attractive than the moment we met.

"After the attack, what did you see?"

He shivered. "Nothing, I — I helped Gloria out of her seat and ran for the door." His demeanor changed. "We're talking about suing. They shouldn't have been locked. That's against codes." He rotated his neck and squeezed his shoulder.

I ignored his threats since the Consociation would likely subsidize settlements for non-disclosures. "What did you see of the next attack, or the attacker?"

He shrugged with a wave of his hands. "I was trying doors, not playing some jackass hero. The crowd was behind me, pushing." Again, he massaged his shoulder.

"Did you ever see the attacker or victims again?"

"No. The door two down from the one we were working on opened, and I got out. I should have left there and then with some of the others, but I did my duty and told the manager what had happened."

"What did he say?" I reached for my phone, ready to close the interview.

"Nothing. He was running past, toward the room or maybe the guard who fell."

The guard had been trampled, according to the reports. "Alright. The agent will have your phone, and you'll be given explicit instructions including a number to call if you remember any other relevant information."

As I escorted him into the hallway and sent him to the FBI, I grabbed a few of Tomas's reports while I waited for the next witness. Digging through everything might take me an hour or two.

My next interview took a good bit longer, as the woman had been on the fringe of the crowd and witnessed all of the attacks. She'd been easier to work with, though she appeared as tired as I was. By the end, she'd begun wringing her hands. These witnesses would never forget the zombie. I'd seen in follow-up reports that they might begin to rationalize what they'd seen to make it conform to their perception of reality.

According to Tomas, none of the witnesses had any direct connection to Iliodor or were witches. Only a few rose to the lowest level of arcane users who had dabbled with past life regressions or tarot.

When I brought her out to the hall, Marie was standing at the opposite side talking with a pinched-faced man. Perhaps two feet taller than her, he wore a dark coat that reminded me of something you'd wear in London and a black fedora without any frills. It wasn't Leah, I assumed. I remained at my door, ready for another interview.

The agent who had been bringing my witnesses gestured that we were done. I paused awkwardly. It didn't feel right to approach Marie in the middle of her conversation. I yawned and fought the temptation to go back in my room to sit in a chair or stretch out across a row of them. I turned on my comms, then scrolled my emails, trying to prioritize the more important reports.

After one email, Marie finished her conversation with the man. He headed for a side exit, and she marched toward me. I put my phone in my pocket and smiled. "I take it that wasn't Leah?"

"No. Public relations — they've got a nightmare on their hands, worse than the rave. They know they can't hamper my investigation, or they'll have more to deal with. We work politely together."

Consociation had a public relations arm? Of course they did. "Do I get to meet Leah?"

"She left already. I'm calling it for the night. We'll get to the employees and Jennifer Siregar's apartment in the morning. Did you come up with anything?"

I shook my head. "Nothing new. I think between the video and these interviews, we've got a solid view of what happened in the room. I read a couple of Tomas's reports. The loss of the camera network here is hindering us. Who locked the doors?"

"I'm hoping the employees and security can help with that." Her tone bristled, and I imagined she still held a grudge against the local police who released them.

A door opened, and an older woman giggled as David let her out. He motioned to her for our benefit, then wiggled his phone in the air. He strode toward us with his smile.

"Anything we can use from the interviews?" Marie asked.

David held up his phone. "Three phone numbers, but they don't help the case much. When will we be done tonight?"

"Tomas, any word on Jennifer Siregar's apartment?" She motioned for us to follow to the escalators.

"No, Pyre. Agent Carlson hasn't reported anyone attempting entry."

"Let Carlson know we'll be there in the morning."

"Already done." He monitored our conversation and acted when she mentioned it earlier.

"Did the FBI come up with anything on the sniper?"

"Agent Carlson wanted to talk with you, remember? Maybe she had an update."

"Damn. Is she still on site?"

There was a silent pause. "Yes. She'll meet you at the front entrance."

"Thanks, Tomas."

We reached the top of the escalator, and Marie scanned around us and downstairs. "We've got rooms at the same hotel as Finn. How's he doing?"

"He'd just woken up when I left. He's got pizza." I planned on checking in on him since I had a key card. Hopefully he'd be sleeping.

Agent Carlson's footstep echoed as she jogged for the escalator. Marie nodded. "We'll be up early, unless Tomas gets a flag on the lich. Be ready to go if I call."

I started to put my phone away. "What should I do with this amulet?"

She turned with a tight focus. "Hold onto it; on your person until we can get it to the vault."

It would be important not to lose it. I'd have to find it in the database when this case was over.

Agent Carlson took the escalator steps two at a time. Her blond hair still appeared neatly tied back. Mine had frizzed with the weather. I'd do what I could tonight and in the morning to get it back in shape.

She spoke before she reached the top. "We believe we have the sniper's perch. No shells, but I've got enough details to be confident. We backtracked the bullet's angle to a two-story window of a school." Agent Carlson gestured behind her. "Fresh marks on an air vent. We have a maintenance worker who let in a workman for air conditioner maintenance, though none had been scheduled. The description was a middle-aged white male with dark glasses and a baseball cap with no logo, possibly gray or blue. High visibility vest."

"Thank you, Agent Carlson. Can you email the report to our office?"

"I did. A Stacey Lockhart had the report a few hours ago."

Marie's face didn't flicker. "If you wouldn't mind also sending it to Tomas, I would appreciate that."

The agent frowned, then nodded. "Of course. We don't have any ID at this point."

"Understood. Thank you. We're heading out for the night. We'll want the site on lockdown for another day, in case Stacey didn't mention that."

Agent Carlson swallowed. "She didn't."

"Thank you. Have a good night." Marie turned and headed for the door. Based on her brisk pace, I guessed she was pissed.

She waited until we were at the Hummer to swear. "Dancing Monkeys."

I had hoped that the ride to the hotel might be less traumatic, but I gripped my pack to my chest as we sped through wet streets, which luckily had little traffic. David made a couple of quips, but we ended up driving in silence.

When I returned to the lobby with a rifle case draped over my shoulder, I got more attention from the employee at the front counter. Marie and David got their keys and took off for the elevator ahead of me.

"Kristen Winters." I handed the man my ID and smiled.

His kept glancing at the weapon case as he processed my cards, then my vest and jacket. "Welcome. The, erm, elevators are right there."

I had cards in multiple pockets now. "Thank you. I'm going to visit my friend before I head up."

His eyes widened a little, as if I might have some nefarious meaning to my statement. "Okay."

Finn was awake and texting when I went in. Dowlin snored from the adjacent room.

"You look better." Sounding clear headed, Finn tossed his phone on his bed. There was a crutch next to him. He followed my eyes. "Yeah. Dowlin wants me moving, but I'm not allowed to put pressure on my leg."

"I look better?"

The pizza boxes were gone, and water bottles were neatly arranged on the nightstand. "Yeah, less fuzzy." He offered an easy grin. "Thanks." Finn nodded at his go bag. "Can you toss the rucksack on my bed? Anything come out of the interviews? I didn't see much in the reports, but I'm still moving slow."

I walked around the bed and put his bag close to where he sat. "Nothing new. There should be a report coming in your email on the sniper. FBI found a roof where they believe he was shooting from."

"Good. How's Leah working out?"

I shrugged. "I don't know. Haven't met her."

Finn opened his bag and began pulling out clothes. Having half a pant leg missing probably bothered his OCD, but the cast wouldn't allow much more. His phone dinged with a message. "I was thinking that the lich never used Earth magic. It could be they never figured out how. They've got mad Haven skills, though. There are some good wards out there for Haven."

"Would it help with a blinding light?"

He turned up to me and grinned, dreads swinging. "I know, right? Couldn't hurt." His phone let out another ding.

"Gary coming out?" I knew he would; when was really the question.

"Marie has him on a 6 a.m. flight." Finn pointed to his phone. "He needs to sleep."

The clock in his room said 11:19 p.m. It would be after 8:00 p.m. where Jade was. "I'm going to get out of these clothes and call my daughter. Feel better."

He glanced at his gun case on my shoulder. "See you in the morning. What time is Marie doing breakfast?"

"Should you be up — early. I'll call or text when I know." I remembered how awkward it had been when Finn and David went on interviews without me in Tallahassee.

My room was on the third floor, at the far end from the elevator. Even without Finn's go bag, my arms ached. I stepped inside and pulled a spell from Mer to close the curtains. The magic took more effort than it should have. I yawned, dumped my load onto my bed, and started calling Jade. The cabinet had a coffee maker with paper cups, so I grabbed one as the phone rang her cell.

"Mom." Jade's tone was noncommittal, but at least not panicked or adversarial.

"Hi, Honey, how are you feeling today?" I peeled the plastic off the cup, trying not to be noisy.

"Okay." There was a pause as she took a slow inhale. "You're not taking me seriously. My warning. You're on a case, aren't you?"

Ear pressing the phone against my shoulder, I didn't fill my cup at the sink, but took a second to respond. Her vision had been of me stuck in Tarus. With a lich involved, I couldn't say it was impossible. "I am taking it seriously. I've been very careful."

I filled my cup as I waited for her to reply. Ever since her vision of me, we'd not been able to have a regular conversation, as awkward as those were at her age. I drank, grimacing at my hair in the bathroom mirror.

I'd filled a second cup before Jade spoke. "It hurts."

"What does, Honey?"

"Worrying about you. I try to forget . . ."

What? That I existed or the job I had? My throat thickened and I put down the cup, moving away from my reflection back out to the bed. "I appreciate that you care, Honey. I do. What I do helps people. I can't tell you about it, but I wouldn't do it if it didn't."

"I know." Her response was choked in a sob, breaking my heart. "I've got to go, Mom."

The connection broke, and I stood staring at my go bag with my cell still against my ear. My lip tugged, but I refused to cry. I didn't have it in me. In summer, I'd visit Jade. Marie would understand.

Blinking, I texted Yaz a quick question and then peeled off my clothes. My hair would do better if I took care of it in the morning, so I set an alarm with barely six hours to sleep. We'd have an early start, and I wanted to spend some time with Finn and then see Jenny's apartment. The case was cooling, but I didn't think it would stay that way.

I was brushing my teeth when Yaz texted two images. Thanking her, I left the phone on the charger, put the Talking Heads on, and dug in my go bag for my pens.

With a silver marker, I began copying her ward for Haven on the inside of my vest.

CHAPTER

EIGHT

The next morning came too quickly. Feeling like a zombie, I drank coffee in the room before fixing my hair and barely getting dressed in time for Marie's call. David was in the hallway outside Finn's room when I rounded the corner from the elevator.

"Beautiful morning, isn't it?" He rattled his mints.

The barely risen sun was stuck behind clouds. "Lovely. Since when are you a morning person?" My go bag felt heavy even without the clothes.

"I'm an all-the-time person." David posed with a handsome smile as he rapped on Finn's door. It was propped open, and he knew it.

"It's open!" yelled Marie from the inside.

David pushed the door, bowing slightly and motioning for me to go first.

Marie sat in an easy chair by the window. "You can't tell when a door is open?"

My mouth opened and I glanced back at a smirking David. I apologized, knowing I'd been played. "Sorry."

She gestured to the menu on the bed. "Pick something."

Finn was propped up against three pillows at his headboard and had replaced his slacks with a pair cut down one side so it fit his air splint. He grinned harder as I raised my eyebrows. "It's not the best option, but it'll work for now."

The door to Dowlin's room was closed. "Sleeping?"

Finn glanced at David who shrugged and spoke. "I'm not a favorite among the dwarves."

"Or anybody," added Marie. "I don't think you'll like anything on the menu, David."

"No mimosa or steak tartare?"

She pointed me toward the menu a second time. It had a simple fare, so I picked a cheese omelet. Before I could say anything, she pointed me at the room's phone. "Two sides of bacon, well done. Black coffee."

Finn tilted his head. "Pancakes and eggs. No meat. Sweet tea."

David ordered hot tea while I was in the middle of the call. Marie started relaying a report that showed a hidden connection between the zombie, Jenny, and Iliodor. When I glanced over at her, she was watching me.

"Unrelated to the case, perhaps, is the death of one of the employees in a head-on collision on his way home last night. A guard named Bill Jackson. There is one other employee who hasn't checked in, Suzanne Wainwright. She works maintenance. I'm trying to decide if we prioritize her over Jenny's apartment."

Since David was standing, I grabbed the desk chair. "The blocked door at the service entrance makes me sure we're looking for an employee. Suzanne might be the one." With the lich missing, a new lead would be helpful.

Marie agreed with a nod and tapped on her comms; hurriedly, I did the same. "Tomas, where are the residences of Jenny Siregar and Suzanne Wainwright in comparison to each other and our location?"

He tapped a keyboard in the background. "Jenny's apartment is near you, two minutes away, Pyre. Suzanne lives twenty minutes away, and her last cell location pinged at her residence. I have no indication she's left. I've got confirmations that everyone else will report to the convention center within the next two hours, even though they had to cancel three multi-room events today. Should I send Leah there to interview them?"

"Yes, thank you."

"Gary has checked in for his flight, Pyre."

Half an hour later, after an expedited meal, we were back in the Hummer where it felt especially empty in the oversized back seats without Finn. Part of me had expected Leah to be traveling with us.

Jenny Siregar had lived in one of a row of five two-story brick apartment buildings. Litter decorated the dead grass by the road, and the parking lot between two buildings had an overflowing dumpster that reeked. The stairs up to her residence were steel and reminded me more of a fire escape than a front entrance. Tomas had alerted the local FBI watching the entrance to our arrival, so they were standing outside their tinted SUV when we arrived. Considering the condition of most of the other cars in the lot, their presence had no doubt been conspicuous.

"Have the FBI hold back, Tomas. I'll speak to them after we're done."

The clouds dampened the sun from breaking through, but they weren't raining and hinted at easing their grip on the day soon. Blue sky peeked from the north where the breeze came from.

The stairs proved worse than I thought as they creaked under our combined weight. David reached for the door, but Marie stopped him. "I'll want prints." She jerked a thumb back at the FBI.

Marie motioned me toward the door, and I grasped a pinch of blue-green ripples to create an unlocking spell. Closely related to a lifting spell, the stream flowed into the cracks, and I could feel where to twist. The locks clicked, and with a second lifting spell, I opened the door.

The stench of death hit us before we were two steps inside.

"Well, we know it happened here," I said, tugging at Dur-Alf to check for wards. "Clear, so far."

The kitchen and living room were tidy, almost devoid of personalization, but obviously used with a teapot on the stove and a bowl and spoon in the sink.

"How much room would a witch need for a zombie ritual?" asked Marie.

"I don't know exactly, but I would think the bedroom would work." I hated breathing since we entered.

David moved for a door, and I quickly tugged on Dur-Alf again to check for wards. "Door's clear," I said, then opened it with a lifting spell.

Jenny's bedroom was still neat and sparse, though a bit more personal. There were no wards, and the small bed had been made with pleasant pale blue sheets. The darker curtains were drawn, but the green-shaded lamp by her bed had been left on. I admired her taste in paintings, though all were landscapes and not hung with the best utilization of her wall space.

"She keeps it pretty clean," said David. The bathroom door was open, and he leaned in.

I tested the next door with Dur-Alf as David approached it and twisted the knob with a lifting spell before he reached for it. I chilled at the sight inside. "Wait."

Runes covered the floor. None were Dur-Alf wards, and the flourishes spoke of Tarus. Marie peered around David and spoke. "So, we're dealing with an arcane user, not a witch."

That made me feel better, but my skin still prickled. "I don't know the arcane ritual for creating a zombie, but there appears more here than I would expect is necessary. I wouldn't go in without studying this."

"David, move back." I couldn't tell if she said it because he might be foolhardy or she wanted a better view. "Tomas, we're sending you pictures. Don't complain about the quality."

David strolled past me back into the bedroom, so I edged up beside Marie. Jenny's altar had been moved from the middle of the room against the window curtains. A dark stain, the source of the foul odor, created an amorphous shape in the center of the floor. The only light in the room was one of three in the fan on the ceiling. Iliodor's known mark, a bisected diamond with a tail continuing down and three circles in the top right, figured prominently on a flag on the far wall. Chimes, feather clusters, and other miscellaneous talismans hung from the other walls. Her pentagram and circle had been marked with painted black runes. The dedications on her altar had been knocked over, and some were even swept under it against the wall.

Marie took a picture of Iliodor's mark. "You're still sure this has nothing to do with Iliodor?"

"We knew she had connections." I studied the painted floor. The space in the center was big enough to hold the body. The runes circling it appeared valid. Four other sigils had been painted into the corners, including at the door; those were the ones that worried me. I took a picture. "Would you be okay with me sending this to an expert?"

Like the central circular set of runes, the grouping had a distinctly Tarus feel to it.

"Yaz?" Marie barely glanced at my phone.

My face heated. Of course, Tomas and the Consociation would know my past. Everything about me. Lovers and mentors. "Yes. Other than my grandmother, who's passed, Yaz has the widest knowledge of anyone I know, and she doesn't ask questions."

"Send it to Tomas first."

I stepped back and opened our secure email. My face remained warm. He'd heard the whole exchange. The air still stunk, and I hated that I was getting used to it. Sending the email, I watched Marie as she continued taking pictures, then focused on the stain in the center.

For a zombie to be created and move, the ritual had to occur immediately after the death. The brain had to retain basic memories such as walking and cognition of objects. Fluids leaked out readily.

"It's been a couple of days since she died." I stated the obvious, but my mind needed to talk it out.

"Yes." Marie typed, prepping her email.

"How did they get the body out of this apartment and to the site?" I asked.

David rattled mints behind me. "Invisible."

I turned, facing him. "Yes, but did they walk there, or drive? The arcane user had to have been the one who moved her."

"Or someone working with him. Maybe the same person who barred the doors at the scene." Marie's comment made sense, and I rearranged cards in my mind. She wouldn't let go of Iliodor, and I couldn't dismiss the possibility entirely, though it meant he'd changed his behavior.

"Close it, lock it." Marie waved her hand at the door.

I pulled a lifting spell from Mer and pulled it closed, then locked it with Dur-Alf. "Forty-eight or more hours ago, someone killed Jenny, painted the runes, and turned her into a zombie. In the next twenty-four, probably yesterday morning before the seminar, they got her to the convention center."

"To meet up with the lich," continued Marie.

"Coordinating with the sniper. Who had to have been hired days prior to scope out his perch."

She gestured toward the front door. "This took some planning."

"Also, someone willing to expose the darker side of the craft and the arcane."

Marie offered me a deadpan stare. "Move it."

I continued speaking even as I led the way to the door. "Iliodor speaks against summoning out of Tarus as the barrier to having the general public accept magic. He has written the Consociation multiple essays pleading them to constrict their activities to that one measure."

"I know what he wrote. He'll do anything to meet his goals. Tomas, do we have Jenny's timeline mapped out? She missed work three days ago, right?"

Tomas swore. "What I have was in my emails."

I cringed at having missed it. There had been so many reports, too much magic, and not enough sleep. When I stepped outside I took a deep breath, ignoring the scent of garbage.

Across the parking lot in the next building, a shape in the window on the bottom floor shifted, disappearing behind curtains. "We should interview the neighbors; maybe they saw our arcane user enter." I started down the stairs, holding the railings though they'd likely collapse with the steps.

"Agreed. After we check on Suzanne Wainwright."

"Do we have time for just one?" I focused on the window, sure I could see the reflection of a lens.

"Okay. Quick."

When we reached the bottom, I led us across the parking lot with the two FBI watching us. David's stride brought him alongside me halfway. "I hope this one's more interesting than Jenny."

"Stow it, David. Tomas, clear the FBI to trace what they can in Jenny Siregar's apartment, but tell them not to enter the closed room."

The elderly white woman who answered held her glasses in her hand. "What's going on? Who are you?" The edges of her wrinkled lips nearly smiled when she focused on David.

"Special Agent Kristen Winters." I showed her my badge, then pointed to Jenny's apartment. "We're trying to locate a missing person from that apartment."

"The hippy chick? Haven't seen her. What'd she do?" The woman's eyes were sharp and focused.

"Just missing. Friends are worried. Did you see anyone enter her apartment a couple days ago?"

The woman smiled slyly. "Mr. Red Corvette? Of course I did. All fancy with his top down and white seats. Wearing one of those big brim hats. He was quite the style to look at. I didn't think she had it in her."

Marie spoke beside me. "Thank you. I'm Special Agent Marie Pyre, and you are?"

"Pyre, what kind of name is that?" The elderly woman frowned, appearing ready to close the door.

David tugged at my elbow, and I let him step forward, flashing a stunning smile and bringing one to the old woman's face. It took him only seconds to pull Mrs. Dimitri's name from her and get us an invite inside. At least she offered tea instead of lime juice. Other than our suspect being a white male wearing a short-sleeved blue shirt and having very firm butt cheeks, we got nothing more out of her. His car had been there when she went to bed at 10:00 p.m. and had been gone in the morning. It would have taken a couple hours to paint all those runes.

When we stepped outside, we saw the FBI had brought in a second team, and they were dusting the stairs and Jenny's door.

"Good catch," Marie said. "Tomas, you get all that?"

I smiled.

"I'm running red corvettes in the area with white interior, two matches so far and both excluded, Pyre."

"Keep at it. Tomas, text David Suzanne Wainwright's address." She led us back to the Hummer. "I'm assuming you'd let me know, but any evidence of Lich?"

Tomas just swore.

David skipped up a step. "I think I caught it with that last shot."

"We didn't find it outside."

"Crawled off somewhere to die — again."

"Last thing we need. I need that body."

I frowned, unsure. "Why?"

"A lich doesn't just do what it's told. Maybe a demon or jinn could compel it. It would require a controlling talisman tied to the summoning ritual, which could give us a lead to Iliodor."

"Or whoever else is controlling it." I cleared my throat without turning toward her.

"You're right. Keep at it."

I held back a flare of self-righteousness. We both had to be open minded. Whoever we were dealing with might not be done, which meant Marie could still be at risk. Being smug wouldn't keep me on my toes. Suzanne Wainwright might lead us to a clue. There were still too many missing pieces.

Tomas spoke rapidly over the comms. "I just got word from Carlson's people." He sounded excited. "Video disruptions at the convention center point to internal sabotage — physical inhibitors, not something I could identify online. They've sent me the images, and we're both searching for the manufacturers. I'll let you know if it leads to anything."

I climbed in the back of the Hummer. Someone had to know technology well enough to plan for those. What didn't they want us to record?

It was only a few minutes before we were driving northwest out of the city into a more rural section of North Carolina.

I still had the images and stench of Jenny's apartment flashing in my head. "Where were Jenny's clothes?" I asked. "I saw nothing discarded. She might have had a hamper." I kept mine in my closet.

"Where are you going with this?" Marie asked.

"There was no reason for her to be naked at the murders. Yet, she was. I can't imagine she answered the door to her killer nude. The ritual doesn't require it that I know of. I'm guessing they were removed afterward, but I doubt either the victim or killer was concerned about hiding them. Otherwise, the altar room would have been scrubbed."

"So maybe in transit," David added. "I personally like to get naked in cars, with the right kind of people."

I ignored him. "If making the zombie naked was for dramatic effect, maybe it happened at the convention center, or in transit."

"Tomas, can you check with Carlson to see if she found any clothes? Have her check the trash bins. Dumpster too." Marie glanced in the rear-view mirror and flashed a smile. "It'll help us pin down a timeline."

Despite being less than useful after the blinding light, I still felt like I'd been adding to the investigation. Odd little bits tugged at me about this case. The failed encounter had left Finn hurt, and we'd lost the lich.

I texted Finn. "How are you feeling?"

"Bored and sore."

"When does Gary get there?"

"An hour. How's it going?"

"Little leads, nothing major. I'm surprised you're not on comms."

"Carlson's people found mine where I got hit. They'll get it to me eventually."

About 8:30 a.m., after spending most of the time texting with Finn about Jenny's apartment, Marie pulled off the highway and entered a winding mess of roads. I spent the next part of the ride holding onto the armrest to stay upright in my seat. The homes we passed were sparse, older, and set back from the road for the most part.

Suzanne Wainwright's black Honda Civic sat by the side of her little white house. The last three digits of the license plate matched what I'd remembered from Tomas's report. The air smelled fresh, and the sun peeked under the clouds to shine over a worn roof. The leafless tree out front was old, and its roots dominated much of the brown yard as they rose above the dirt.

"Haven," Marie suggested as I joined her outside the Hummer.

The house was tiny enough that it would probably give me good visibility, though I moved closer to get the sun out of my eyes. I tugged into Haven, and the life detection spell gave no indication of anyone home. I shook my head and stepped up on the first of the two rickety steps.

Marie passed me and rapped loudly on the door. She glanced back at me, and I shook my head again. The curtains, old and faded to a cream color, were closed and didn't allow us to see inside.

"Nothing." Haven showed no indication of life inside except a couple tiny glows under the house that might have been rodents.

Marie knocked again, despite my comment, then motioned for us to walk around the side. An old house, it showed signs of wear and disrepair, but the windows were all covered with curtains or shades. We circled the back and came to the side with Suzanne's well-used car. She had a faded plastic flower on the dash, and the front was clean.

"Well, we might have found Jenny's clothes." I indicated the back passenger window. A pair of sandals and a pile of clothes had been left loose on the floor.

Marie joined me. "Maybe." She circled her fingers in the air, a gesture for me to open the car door with magic.

I tested Dur-Alf first, then drew into Mer to open the unlocked door. As I did so, the rancid stench of death escaped, and I pulled back. "Well, I think we've answered that."

It appeared likely that Suzanne had brought zombie Jenny to the convention building. We might be able to reconstruct more with interviews. Two small pieces of the puzzle had been connected, but they didn't lead us to the lich or who summoned it.

David leaned beside Marie as I stepped back. I expected him to make a snarky comment, but he just nodded toward the house. "We should look inside."

"Agreed. Don't touch anything, same as Jenny's." She tilted her head toward the front door.

I tugged at Dur-Alf, but there weren't any wards. I tested the knob with a simple lift spell from Mer to turn it, but unlike the car, it was locked. I unlocked it and opened the door. Even knowing there was nobody inside, at least alive, my stomach tightened.

The living room was neat with a small sofa, a clean carpet on the wooden floor, and a television on a stand beside the door. I tugged at Dur-Alf again. "It looks clear."

David strode inside with little care, followed by Marie. When I stepped in, I could smell a corpse just over the scent of burned toast.

With the bedroom door open, I checked for wards before we entered. We found Suzanne on her bed with her eyes staring at the ceiling. She wore stained work clothes. Her left arm dangled over the edge of the bed so her wrist and hand hung in the air. Beside her elbow, nestled in the wrinkled coverlet, was a needle. Elastic cut into her arm.

It wasn't as if I hadn't seen an overdose before. I just didn't believe this one, especially with the zombie's clothes in the back seat of Suzanne's car. Tracks were being covered, but not as neatly as they could be. We had no witnesses to interview.

"Well, two employee deaths. The guard Bill was involved, I'd bet." Neither Marie nor David responded.

Marie scanned the rest of the otherwise tidy room. "Tomas, we need Suzanne Wainwright's body picked up at her residence. Have them bag the clothes in her car as well."

"I'll check for an ETA on a retrieval team, Pyre."

"She and Bill had to be compelled. Maybe the sniper too." I waved around the neat bedroom with a small bookcase and a book on her nightstand. There were pictures on the dresser and jewelry tucked in trays and a box. "Tomas never reported any substance abuse with this woman. They were forced to kill themselves. The arcane user who zombi-fied Jenny and likely summoned the lich couldn't do that."

Marie studied me, then pursed her lips before she spoke. "There were times, long ago, when witches and arcane users could compel. We had assumed the knowl-edge lost."

My eyebrows rose. "I've never heard this."

David snorted. "Me neither, and I've lived for a very long time."

She scanned the room. "I would hope there is some other explanation, but we must keep this arcane user alive and learn what they know."

We donned gloves and dug through Suzanne's belong-ings, but found no sign of her being involved with the arcane. According to her file, she'd rented the house a year ago after a nasty relationship ended. Work and a local friend had been the extent of her social life. Nothing in her residence said otherwise. Spending more time at Suzanne's than we had at Jenny's, I longed to return to her apartment.

As I poked through Suzanne's well-organized but small closet, Tomas broke through on the comms. "Pyre, we've got a transport coming for the body in twenty minutes. Do you want local FBI there?"

"Yes, please. Wait until transport has finished. I'd love to catch a fingerprint on something." Marie spoke from the opposite side of the bedroom; David had moved into the rest of the house.

"Tomas, could you get me a list of other deaths in Winston-Salem and the area? I'm looking for someone who might be the sniper. I think whoever set this up planned on getting rid of any witnesses." I paused as I noticed a flower print dress pulled out from the other clothing hung in the closet. "Thank you."

Finn surprised us all, coming over the comms. "Good idea. I've been going through the reports as quickly as I can, before Gary gets here. Which will be any minute."

"What have you come up with, Finn?" Marie asked.

"Pyre, the depth of the plan has me still stuck with Iliodor, but I agree with Kristen that he wouldn't stoop to using Tarus. It could be one of his followers acting on his own."

"That's a possibility," she said.

Glancing back at Suzanne's body, I pulled down two cardboard boxes of pictures and leafed through them quickly. Tomas's data and our own search did not show a connection between Suzanne and anything related to the arcane or witches. The compelling felt out of place. Even the lich had been well manipulated.

I spoke over the comms without intending anyone specific as my audience. "What if the lich isn't the only cryptid summoned? It's convoluted; however, a demon or jinn could be summoned and controlled, and they could compel the two employees, maybe even Jenny." I immediately thought of the *Ars Goetia*, despite its failings.

Marie paused and faced me. "Controlling either of them would take some skill."

I nodded, perhaps too excited. "As does manipulating a lich, though a talisman could do that. But someone able to create zombies too? This user is knowledgeable." We might be missing something as well.

She'd just started to nod when Tomas broke in over comms, rather excited. "Pyre, I've got a local enforcement alert east of you. An elderly man claims there's someone strange wearing a Halloween costume heading across his property. A kale farm. The police are on their way."

My pulse rose at the thought of facing it again. I drew a steady breath, then closed the closet door. Focusing on

Marie's face, I avoided a glance at the dead woman, another victim and pawn in all this. We couldn't do much more than try and stop any further deaths.

"Squash their investigation and get us a location sent to David's phone." As she spoke, she gestured for me to hurry behind her, and her sudden brisk walk made my chest tingle.

I didn't particularly want to engage the lich again after the damage Finn had taken, but we needed to. David had beaten us to the door and held it open, letting in fresher air.

"What do we do about the lock?" I asked, following last.

"Close it. Don't lock it. They'll be here in a minute."

There was a quiet house across the street with a more manicured yard, and on our side of the street, a deserted, ruined building next door appeared as if it were built a century ago. No one seemed interested in what we were doing. The clouds had cleared, and it felt like it might warm up.

Marie stormed toward the car. "Tomas, where are we with the local officers at the farm? Have they pulled back?"

"Negative, Pyre. Stacey is in contact with their department." His high-pitched voice shifted. "In regards to deaths around Winston-Salem, there are only two others since the shooting. Neither is relevant."

I frowned, trotting behind Marie to the Hummer. "Why not?"

He swore lightly. "Both were medical conditions. A hospitalized gunshot wound prior to the attack, and a hospice patient."

Flushing, I swallowed. "Thanks, Tomas." I climbed into the back, buckled, and dug into my go bag for water. Placing the bottle between my legs, I pulled out my phone and looked at an expanded map of the area. Our present location placed us northeast of Winston-Salem, midway between the scene of the assassination and Greensboro.

Marie dusted the yard as she backed onto the road. David began calling out directions.

Suzanne's location was in the same county as Winston-Salem. "Did you check the whole county, Tomas?"

His curses grew more elaborate. "No. City limits. I'll expand now."

"Thanks." I drank my water and did not glance at the windshield though we were still on back roads. If we could catch up with the lich and stop it, then we would only have the arcane user to deal with.

Marie pulled onto a small highway. "Tomas, has Stacey pulled the locals?"

"No, Pyre. Three units are on the property and a canine in transit. I'm tracking communications, but there's no sign of the intruder. I don't have anything on social, but it is very rural there. North of Greensboro."

"Dancing monkeys. If that lich attacks, this is on Stacey." Marie gunned the Hummer, and I focused on my feet. I wanted to ask about the Corvette driver, but opened my email instead and tried to read reports. I know they'd said that Marie's dragon senses helped us avoid dying on the road, but it was easier to believe if I didn't see any of our near misses. The swerving and horns were enough. We had a good twenty minutes for me to focus on Tomas's reports, and I barely glanced out the windows the entire time.

No updates came in on the lich in the kale fields, so perhaps it had been coincidence or a random sighting. We could have a lot worse going on if the lich were still in Winston-Salem or a surrounding urban area and coming here was a mistake. We didn't have one solid lead.

Before we pulled down a dirt road, the last sign I spotted pointed toward I-75. We jerked to a stop between a squad car and an SUV with a Guilford County Sheriff's insignia. I eased out a breath as I unbuckled and climbed out of the Hummer. Hints of soil and new growth hung in the air. The farm spread along a wide strip with a small set of barns and a worn house at the center edge. Curtains hung at the windows, blocking any view inside.

The adjacent property was similar. There weren't many places to hide, except for the brush that grew up on the outer edges of the newly planted green rows. A small copse of trees offered little in the way of cover. Had the sun not been out, it might have appeared different.

Even as Marie began questioning the local sheriff, Tomas spoke on the comms. "I've got something, Kristen." I couldn't remember him saying my name before. "Military vet shot by police. Drunken or disoriented and brandishing a 9mm as he approached them and fired."

"Suicide by cop," I said, watching Marie and David speak to two relaxed officers with matching salt and pepper mustaches.

Marie paused, noticeably glanced at me, then continued her conversation at the edge of the short kale field. I really hoped we weren't going to take a walk in it.

Local enforcement had been here for a quarter of an hour, but already they appeared at ease. There had been no sign of the lich since the farmer's original sighting, or they would have been more focused. The pair I could make out in the field appeared to be returning. I saw distant figures at the end in a line of trees with what appeared a canine.

Tomas spoke over the comms even as Marie engaged the local officers, but his speech was slower and almost timed to mesh. I focused on his words. "The man who died is Reg Simpson. Ex-military with long-range weapon experience. The locals searched his apartment. They have confiscated a burner phone and unusual ammo along with his weapons."

"Unusual ammo. Sniper's rifle?" I asked.

He paused. "No, but notably a rifle missing from his gun rack. It's mentioned in their report."

Marie turned, finishing her conversation and walking toward me as she spoke quietly into her comms. "Send local FBI to retrieve the ammo and phone. Get me an address; I want to see this residence."

I hadn't been paying much attention to her discussion with the local officers. Were we staying and searching, or moving on? From her annoyed march, I assumed we were heading off to investigate the possible sniper.

Pausing, I turned slowly and found the scenario unusual. How had the lich passed through so much territory, only to be spotted here?

"Which way had it been heading?" I asked Marie.

"East." She didn't break stride, heading for the Hummer. "The county just put up a helicopter in that direction, moving in on this location. We'll know in ten minutes if they find something. Tomas, link up with them."

"Got it, Pyre."

I headed for my door as I spoke. "So, until something new comes in, we track the ammo and cell phone leads and check the potential sniper's residence."

Marie climbed into the driver's seat. "Exactly."

TEN

I dug into our secure email and scrolled through reports as we sped down dirt roads and cut back to the paved highway. Marie drove with a vengeance, though I wanted to dig into the possible sniper's evidence as well. One of these leads had to bring us back to the red corvette driver who I assumed was the arcane user who'd been at least part of this.

Leah had been filing interview reports on the employees who hadn't died. I could see where her questions turned toward what the others had noticed of any behavioral change with Suzanne or Bill. Meeting her would be interesting, if we ever returned to Winston-Salem. The morning had turned into more driving than I anticipated, and I'd be asking for a pee break soon.

My comms crackled as Finn spoke. "Hey, Gary's here. I'm going off comms for a bit, but I'll check email regularly." He sounded more apprehensive than excited. Gary would be upset.

"I'll text later, Finn." I wish I could be there with them. Gary responded well when the three of us talked about work issues. I'd been through the same with my ex and Jade. "Tell Gary hi. Good luck."

It was a few minutes after turning west on another rural highway when Tomas alerted us to second sighting of the lich even farther east than the kale farm. "I've intercepted the calls to local enforcement. You're thirty minutes out. Three FBI agents have been diverted to hold the scene for us, and they'll be there in fifteen."

David held up his phone. "I've got the map. We'll need to turn around."

I lost a snack bar out of my go bag when we did a U-turn on the road. Marie spoke calmly. "Air surveillance?"

"They've got nothing in the air, Pyre. I've requested a flight out of Greensboro. Got a call into Durham as well."

"Details?"

"Two boys on ATVs followed a 'creepy guy in robes' onto their neighbor's property, where he entered the open garage and disappeared. They called 911, which I was monitoring, so I yanked the call. They've returned to their residence, a nearby farm, and have no video on their phones."

"Homeowners?"

"Not answering their cell phones, no land lines."

If the local FBI wouldn't get there for fifteen minutes, then the lich could move on and we'd be wasting our time, again. I knew we didn't have a choice; we had to pursue the lead.

A half an hour later, with one very bounced and full bladder, I tensed as we skidded onto a gravel drive beside a fat evergreen. The drive, more of a dirt road with some leftover gravel, disappeared into a dreary forest thick with bramble, though the trees were mostly leafless. I assumed, hoped really, there was a building at the end. At least it was daylight.

"Where are the agents?" I asked.

"Monitoring the exits to the residence."

"Any activity?" asked Marie.

"Not since they arrived, Pyre."

"It seems strange," I said. "Running all this way from Winston-Salem — where's it going? Then visible a couple of times, the last alert when it is seen going into a building."

"Could be a trap." Marie didn't sound concerned.

"Why here?" I glanced up to see a black SUV parked ahead, but trees blocked any buildings.

"Tomas, any connections with the occupants?"

"Nothing, Pyre. Father, Terrence Flowers, and his son, Robert, are both heavily involved in a local Baptist church. No arcane or witch connections."

We raced up the drive and cleared the edge of the winter woods. At the far end of a dried lawn, a man in a dark suit shifted. "The residents aren't responding to calls?" Someone would have tried to reach them.

Tomas sighed, slightly exasperated, but at least not swearing. "They don't answer. No activity on either phone all day. Neighbors must have heard of the activity and left messages, as did I."

The FBI had parked far up the drive, and Marie tore through the grass around it. A second man stood deep in the yard to our left, halfway to a newly plowed field. A sprawling single-story house with faded brickwork at the front door had newer sections with pale blue siding. The attached two-car garage was white and a recent addition. A hint of screen at the back corner suggested a porch. I didn't see the third agent; perhaps they were on the opposite side of the house.

"Wait," I said. "Is it unusual for these people not to use their phones all day?"

Marie glanced in the mirror toward me as she drove straight ahead, bringing us to the front of the house. "What's your concern?" We lurched to a stop. Two work trucks were parked by the front door.

The garage had benches for work, not storage. "Tomas said there hasn't been any activity on their phones all day. That might be normal for some people, or not." I hustled to get my seat belt off.

Tomas swore. "Pyre, it is unusual, for the son at least. Robert Flowers hasn't responded to any social media or messages since 8:07 this morning. He is usually active multiple times within an hour. It's been almost three hours."

I hopped out to join Marie, and she motioned us forward. "I get it," she said. When she twitched her fingers, I assumed she wanted me to search for life with Haven. "It's likely a trap."

David strode from the far side of the Hummer and caught up with us. The two FBI agents watched us cautiously. The house was too large and the sunlight too bright for a spell from Haven to be effective, but we had to try. My chest tightened as I tugged at the fluffy white realm. Finn behind us with the rifle would have been a little more comforting.

Marie aimed for the open garage, where the lich had been seen entering. Smaller animals were nesting under the foundation, and birds clustered in brush on the far side. "I'm not picking up anything in the garage or just inside the house."

"How far can you see?" asked Marie.

"Well, that's the problem. I can't really tell how far it's working until something shows up."

As he reached the garage bay entrance, David rattled mints, and Marie shushed him. The shop smelled like grease and oil, nothing dead. An old wooden door at the back left was closed. Haven didn't highlight any life inside. I tugged at Dur-Alf but didn't find any wards. Small engines and parts cluttered most of the corners and benches. The wall against the house had been shingled wood, and shelves had been built against it. Ragged cardboard boxes filled every inch.

David reached the single step leading to the door, drew his weapon, and glanced back at me.

"Nothing," I said. Pulling a lift spell from Mer, I opened the door for him, not that I thought the lich would leave useful fingerprints.

He took one step onto the threshold, paused, and waved us closer. "What a waste. It's all dried up."

The stench of old blood wafted into the garage. Dark red painted the floor and refrigerator. Chunks of flesh lay strewn in unidentifiable shapes. Little light came in from the curtained window above the sink to highlight the carnage. David's body glowed with Haven, so I knew my spell still worked, but the rest of the house was dark.

I stepped back. "Well, this happened before the lich arrived, I would bet. If there's anything deeper inside, it's not showing in my vision." With a shrug, I gestured to David and the animals outside the garage. "The Haven spell is working, though."

Marie studied the bloody kitchen, then motioned us around to the front of the house. "Front door."

I spun out spells, tugging at Dur-Alf to check for wards, resetting the Haven detection, and unlocking then opening the front door. My pulse held a steady pace, though nothing lurched out at us. No blood waited in the living room, and beyond David's glow and a few critters under the house, I saw nothing alive inside. The couch smelled like beer and chips, though the room was surprisingly neat for a father and son. The television blocked most of the light from the front window.

Standing in the center between the couch and front door, I could make out the blood splatter from the kitchen onto the wood floor of the living room. A dark mangled shape rested partially in a hall that led to the back of the house off of the kitchen. It was the only access to the rear of the building.

David peeked into a room to our left. "Bedroom. What are we looking for, Pyre?" He gestured across the living room toward the kitchen. "Now that we've found that." Glancing back at me he raised his eyebrows. "Anything else alive in here?"

I shook my head, cringing as Marie walked toward the bloody kitchen. "Let me see if there's a back door we can come in through," I offered.

She knelt at the edge of the spatter and gestured me outside.

We'd left the front door open, so I quickly exited, trotting down the two steps. The agents I could see to the left and the right watched carefully as I made for the side of the house opposite the garage. The backyard ended in a freshly tilled field with old barns settled at the edge of the woods. The third agent waited fifty feet from the back. A solemn, pale woman in her forties, she studied me without any emotion.

The back patio had newer screening and blue and white furniture. I pulled at Dur-Alf and stopped as I reached the flimsy porch door. It had been left partially open. Blood trailed from under it and into the dried winter grass. The streak led toward the fields.

"Well, we've got something back here." The back door to the house was closed, but a dark red smear trailed across the patio. Fresh air mingled with a hint of old viscera.

"One of the bodies, or part of it, might have been dragged from the house."

The crumbling moss green of Dur-Alf appeared between me and the woods ahead. My fingers had just been tugging at the realm, but this wasn't from me. Reflexively, I yanked a shield out of the realm just in time.

The attempted binding slammed into my magic, and the resulting force sent me to the ground. The binding failed, and I flared out my Dur-Alf shield while reaching for my gun.

"Kristen?" Marie asked.

I rolled to a knee and glanced from the dry forest to the agent who had turned and drawn her weapon. She faced the woods, but unless she were a witch, she wouldn't have seen the realm being used.

"I've got a witch back here." I focused on the leafless trees and dried underbrush, searching for a hint of movement.

A figure burst out in a spray of dried leaves and snapping vines. It raced for the agent, not me. The woman assumed a quick stance and fired rapid shots into the red and gray skinless cryptid.

"Kristen?" Marie sounded more annoyed than worried.

As I drew my weapon and centered on the leaping draugr, a second figure skittered from the woods. Appearing entirely human, it raced away from us into the fresh field. Gun aiming as the draugr closed the last few steps, I let my shield drop and drew my fingers into the Dur-Alf realm.

"A witch and a draugr," I said into the comms.

ELEVEN

I chanced a shot before the draugr reached the FBI Agent, especially as she had taken two quick steps back and continued to empty her magazine. Her movement appeared to confuse the cryptid, forcing it to slow from its preternatural speed and adjust mid-step. I remembered they didn't do well in full light.

My bullet might have been the one that tore at its shoulder, but none of our shots stopped it. Muscle flapped without any hint of blood. I grimaced, foregoing a second shot. Instead, I flung a trail of crumbling Dur-Alf.

The draugr slipped under my badly aimed binding spell and slashed. One vicious clawed hand tore into the FBI agent's jacket and Kevlar, tearing tufts of fabric free. The other ripped open her throat, sending a sudden wash of blood onto the dried grass like spilled paint.

I didn't need to be careful any longer and slammed a second binding spell into the draugr, but it had already started leaping away from the corpse. Unsure of its intended direction, I threw up a shield between us. The spell was too close and broad for me to aim around. From the back of the yard, someone fired, but I couldn't see them. It might have been David and Marie.

My attempted binding slipped off as the draugr launched wildly toward the far side of the house and the gunfire. My heart sped, even as it left me behind. Luckily, I hesitated and left my shield up just long enough. The edge of the witch's spell scraped into it, and the two fragments of Dur-Alf glowed dark green as they crumbled against each other. I had lost track of her, thinking that she'd loosed this draugr upon us and intended to escape. The gun firing from the back of the building had distracted me while she'd stopped at the edge of the field, crouching and whipping binding spells in my direction.

I stepped to the side and pulled my shield cleanly between us. "The witch is at the back field; be careful." Aiming my weapon, I considered flicking my spell aside and taking a shot.

She took the moment to throw up her own shield and race into the field. Most of the tilled earth was surrounded by leafless trees in the distance with an occasional dark smudge of evergreen. Along the left side were two old buildings which might have been abandoned from the growth around them.

Multiple weapons fired from near the garage, and I eased toward the corner of the screened porch, trying to keep an eye on the fleeing witch but searching out the draugr.

"Situation?" called Marie. She and David had followed my path and were coming up behind me.

Dropping my shield, I pointed toward the back of the witch making her way toward the closest of the barns. "Witch." I gestured with my weapon toward the ruckus which was the draugr.

"David, with me. Kristen, cover us."

I swore David rattled mints as he flew by, his weapon drawn. Marie cleared past me, and I kept pace with her, peering back at the fields and the surrounding forest. We still had no sign of the lich. The residents were likely dead long before it had arrived. The draugr and witch had been the trap, though an ineffective one. Using one hand, I tugged at Dur-Alf, searching for wards, and pulled out a shield to throw beside Marie, just in case. She was the target.

David had sped far ahead by the time I rounded the edge of the screened porch. Rapid shots sounded from the front where we'd parked. The second agent had been torn apart and left bleeding close to the edge of the garage. David raced forward even though he might be heading into friendly fire.

I kept my shield hovering near Marie, even as I spun and made sure nothing came at us from the fields or woods. Almost subconsciously, I tugged into Dur-Alf, prepping a binding spell.

David stopped in the front yard, just in my sight, and began firing. His aim changed at each pull of his trigger, and I imagined the draugr, having finished with the last agent, bouncing back toward us.

Gliding my shield forward toward David, I tossed the binding spell blindly in front of him.

I caught the golden glimmer of Salmhalla as Marie's dragon tail appeared from the dead grass beside her, grew, and arched impossibly fast like an arrow. She had a better angle, and I trusted that she could see the draugr approaching David.

Pausing, I flipped the shield so it rolled higher in front of David and covered his head and left side. I let his aim and Marie's tail guide me. The binding spell I targeted at a space yet unoccupied, about chest level and closer to me than the shield.

The draugr's left arm sagged as it leaped into view. Its right claw arched high, intending to rake down David's face, but my teammate never flinched.

I shifted my shield forward the ten inches necessary, and the draugr's nails slammed into hardened air. Its body twisted from the momentum. My binding spell slapped low, about the cryptid's legs, and slowed its velocity. Marie's tail harpooned the draugr through the rib cage, yanking it back from David. The creature flopped from the combined impacts.

David shot the cryptid in the forehead. I would have never had that kind of calm presence to let it almost gore me and maintain my aim.

My binding caught, but it was already dying with most of its skull torn apart. Marie's tail ripped out of its ribcage with gray and red flesh stuck on her barbs. Her appendage moved in a flash but appeared to vaporize even as it did so. My eyes couldn't follow it before it faded from Earth.

I dropped my spells and flicked a glance to the fields behind us. The witch was gone. The three agents were dead. "This is a trap," I said.

"Yeah. Which way did they go?" Marie asked.

I pointed across the field. "That building, I'm guessing." Turning to check on David, my eyes lingered on the mangled agent. "How about the third agent?"

David stood closer to the front and mocked a wincing grimace. "Not a good look. Never wear a white button-down if you're going to get shredded like that." He gestured toward where we had parked. "I'm grabbing some extra ammo. I think we'll need it." In a loping jog, he disappeared from view past the corner of the garage.

I holstered my own weapon and surveyed the cryptid,

mangled agent, and the distant wooden barn. The sun glinted off an edge near a metal roof. The brown brush appeared to have grown up around the building, giving it the sense of abandonment. We'd have to search it. Marie wouldn't bring out any other FBI to get harmed. I recognized that she mainly used them to keep local enforcement or yahoos from entering. Otherwise, she didn't expect them to do more than monitor.

This hunt, or trap, was left to the three of us.

David loped back around and joined us, worrying at a spot of cryptid on his jacket with a handkerchief. "Finn's big gun would be welcome about now."

I agreed, though I didn't know how quickly he'd be on his feet again. We had a new witch to deal with. She might have been the one to pull through a draugr, but she wouldn't be the arcane user. "We might be facing them all," I said, gesturing ahead as we took the first step forward. "Arcane user, lich, and witch. And whatever else they drummed up."

CHAPTER

TWELVE

An earthy, spring scent hung over the field despite the obvious blood trail we were likely supposed to follow. Two pairs of footprints led the way. One could have been the draugr's, and the second, fresher tracks, were the witch's. I ran possible scenarios through my head where the draugr doubled back after dropping off a bloody corpse. It didn't quite make sense yet.

I tugged at Dur-Alf and kept burning a detection spell from Haven in case we met an invisible lich or some such. The last couple days had held more surprises than I appreciated.

We walked a yard away from the side of the tracks, David leading while I kept pace beside Marie who frowned, speaking into her comms. "Tomas, any activity from the gunshots?"

"I've intercepted it all, Pyre. I'm assuming you don't want anyone else involved at the moment."

"Not unless Leah can get here in the next five minutes."

Tomas swore. "Would you like me to get her on the move toward your location? Just in case?"

"Keep Leah with the interviews. We might end up needing another lead. The lich might be here waiting for us, but we're still looking for an arcane user."

David never glanced back. "My corvette man."

"Understood, Pyre. I have the pickup of the bodies on hold until you clear the scene. They are fifteen minutes out when you're ready."

We continued in silence as the trail led directly toward the house. The sky had turned a light blue with the only clouds remaining showing no threat of rain.

Dur-Alf puckered ahead. "David, stop." I shifted around him, tugging at the realm.

An arcane ward was drawn with sigils and runes locking in the intent of the magic from the realm. This ward had been created by a witch like me. The symbols were more intuitive and drawn by the intent of the maker as it affected the realm. In this case, a crushing spell. Arcane magic was an imitation of true craft from a witch.

Standing a few yards away, I tugged at the edge, slowly disrupting the form of the ward. It covered a four-foot diameter and would be triggered upon any physical disruption. If David had stepped at the edge, it would have snapped onto him and attempted to crush him to pulp. I wasn't really sure how that would work out in the end.

As the first symbol deteriorated, the ward crumbled. "Clear."

We were a hundred feet away from the building, and I pulled a shield from Dur-Alf and positioned it in front of us. The sides of the barn were made of warped and stained slats which ran from top to bottom of each floor. It appeared to be at least two floors with a pitched loft rising above that. The door was gone, leaving a gaping rectangle into darkness. Far on the left side, a paned window tilted from settling. Most of the metal roof was rusted.

"Let me lead with the shield; I'm too far away to detect anything with Haven."

Marie nodded, but we ended up walking together in a line toward the barn, with me in the center, holding a shield they couldn't see. She drew her weapon, and David followed suit.

On the far left, there had once been an open section of the barn with an overhang, but dried brush had filled the space. Younger trees had grown close to the walls on all sides except the front edge along the field. Lighter weeds and vines coated the front. The only green came from two pines behind the building. The brown vegetation added to the desolate air of the structure.

The tracks and a second Dur-Alf ward across the threshold of the open doorway made for a strong argument that the barn was, in fact, occupied. "Wait." Holding my shield closer, I pinched into Haven. "I'm picking up one occupant."

A faint ghost of a shape hovered deep in the structure. It gave me a sense of where to keep my shield placed as I approached to tug at yet another crushing spell. Binding wards required more finesse than this witch had demonstrated.

A second figure waited behind the first. "Two. Both in the back." I glanced behind before I edged closer to work on unraveling the ward. David had put on sunglasses. They wouldn't stop Haven light, but he smiled handsomely when I noticed.

The next step brought up more life in the Haven detection, but it was a thin haze in pockets on the floors and walls. It was either insects or rodents, not masses like the two denser forms. Still, I didn't relish the idea of walking through an infestation. "Bugs," I said quietly into the comms as I disarmed the ward.

"What?" Marie asked.

"There's insects in the barn. Lots."

"Will that be a problem?" She sounded more incredulous than concerned.

I blushed. "No." I still kept a shield between me and the darkness.

The ward crumbled along the door's threshold, and I tugged to check for another before stepping closer to the edge. The interior remained shrouded in darkness except for the first couple of feet from the door. Dirt and dust showed two sets of footprints leading in, a couple drops of muddy blood where something had been dragged in, and no sign of the critters that appeared to squirm in lumps. The stale air carried a slightly musty scent, which could have been from David behind me. "I'm worried there might be a second draugr or cryptid here. Two tracks in, none out."

"Back door maybe? However, you did say two inside," suggested Marie. "David, take the lead and be prepared to shoot."

He stepped up beside me, weapon drawn and sunglasses low on the bridge of his nose so he could peer over the top of them at me. "Someone once said, 'Ideas are more powerful than guns.'"

"Perhaps, but arguing the point might be in vein." I grimaced at my sloppy pun, keeping my eyes on the glowing, wriggling masses, then I formed a second shield sending it ahead of David.

Marie pushed past me. "Stow it, both of you."

Holding both shields, I refreshed my Haven detection spell. It was target specific, rather than focused around me, so I tossed it deeper inside and lit up everything a little brighter. The congregations of bugs piled not just on the floor, but along the walls, with thick nests at the upper corners. I'd grown up with old barns in Oregon, and this wasn't a normal infestation.

As I ventured over the threshold, Marie's flashlight lit up, disrupting the hazy view and leaving only the strongest two shapes prominent. "I've still got two, ahead and slightly to the right, no movement." The musty air felt humid.

Her beam of light touched only a short ceiling and a wall to our right, giving us some sense of the massive depth of the barn. David crouched slightly as he walked, waving through spiderwebs. The ceiling appeared greenish, perhaps with mold.

"Smells like Earth magic in here," Marie said.

I would have loved to ask for details, but tugged at Dur-Alf to search for a ward. Juggling the two shields, I kept one between David and the two shapes, though they weren't moving. He grunted as a foot sunk into the ground with a squelching crunch.

Marie flicked her light on his leg. Inch long centipedes were rolling out of the nest. They clung to the cuff of his slacks as he stepped out, shaking his foot. I couldn't pull my eyes away as they climbed up and, I imagined, inside. He didn't flinch or slow as he stepped forward. She brought her light ahead again, but I could see the distinct haze of their shapes wriggling up.

When something dropped into my curls just above my left ear, I squeaked, causing Marie to check on me. Flicking at my hair with one hand, I kept both shields active and in place. Shivers ran down my spine, and I just wanted to smash a hole in the roof and let in some sun. A better option might be a swat helmet; I could use a headlamp then. My hair would be a mess, though.

A third form glided beside the two glowing shapes ahead of us. I recognized the movement. "Lich ahead."

My foot sank half an inch into a nest, and I hopped sideways, bouncing behind Marie. One of the other hazy forms burst toward us with enough speed that I believed it to be a draugr. I shifted the shield in front of David moments before the sound of wood splintered in the darkness. Marie's flashlight beam caught the last shards flying as the gray, skinless cryptid smashed into my Dur-Alf magic and rebounded into shredded wood.

The ceiling creaked from the chaos and activity, which allowed dust to drift and wet drops to drip onto my jacket. David's first shot sunk into my shield and lit up the draugr tearing through broken planks of a thin, mold covered wall. As his second shot fired nearly point blank, the lich lit a ball of Haven light and tossed it at us. Marie's gun flashed as she fired one shot after the next.

The ward I'd drawn against Haven magic did little to ease the effect, but I had a moment to squeeze my eyes shut before the sphere burst against something and lit my eyelids bright red. Leaving both shields up, I scraped a third spell from Dur-Alf and flung a binding spell toward the last place I'd seen the glowing form of the lich.

The blinding after-image hung in my vision. As he shifted, I dropped the shield I'd been holding in front of David. Impaired, I'd not known where to place it effectively. The shield I'd left in front of me, I drew closer and arced over my head. Debris, some of it alive, had been dropping from the ceiling. Left mostly unable to see, I refreshed the Haven detection to brighten the glowing forms. Marie and David were the brightest, except for the draugr, which danced and clawed at my preternaturally quick vampire teammate. The cryptid had slowed; I could only guess from being hit by one of our bullets. I needed to help. The draugr would eventually make a mess of David, even if his vampire metabolism could put him back together.

A fireball blossomed close to Marie. The blast staggered me away, and heat singed my left side where my shield didn't cover. The ceiling smoldered and sparked with the acrid scent of smoke. As I reached for another Dur-Alf shield, a crushing spell slammed me to the insect-infested floor.

The witch was strong. I would have been damaged were it not for the shield I held. If she tucked in a binding spell, or a second crushing spell, I'd be in trouble.

David danced with the draugr. Marie had been far to my left and twisted under a spell, so I couldn't see her. Close behind the cryptid, the witch, a male from his shape, had moved up to the shredded wall. He barely glanced at me, then David, scanning as if searching for Marie. The lich kept farther back in the barn, gliding from one side to the next.

Marie's voice grumbled in the dull ring of her compelling. "Cease."

The witch's crushing attack on me ended, but so did my own shield spell. I was conscious of this, but lacked any ability to protect myself. Emotions felt dulled without any bodily reaction.

The draugr caught David's arm, drawing him close. As the gun fired, I managed a glimmer of satisfaction. The muzzle flash was dulled in the chin of the cryptid, but left enough light for me to see.

Marie's flashlight was gone, but flames gnawed at a drier section of the ceiling. She fired at the lich, and her tail swung about, but the witch and I were left under her compelling. I felt no sense of it to fight against; I merely had no will to do anything.

I did wonder why I'd been affected when David and the now dead draugr had been just as close.

A Haven-derived fireball engulfed Marie and singed my left shoe and pants. I had some gratitude that the ward I'd drawn offered some protection. However, insects found me, and my emotions spiked despite the Salmhalla magic. They crawled over my right hand, between fingers, and under the cuff of my jacket, but I didn't flinch. How long would dragon-shifter compelling last? It did not seem a timid magic, as part of me could still hear the ring of Marie's voice.

David had replaced his magazine. The residual of my Haven detection was fading, but I recognized his movements even in the dull firelight. The acrid smoke added to the haze.

Something crawled over the collar of my suit and tentatively touched my neck. Deep inside of me, some part screamed in rage and panic. I lay there in the moldy dirt as flames licked at the drier parts of the building. If I survived this, which I questioned the likelihood of at the moment, I'd have to sit Marie down and discuss some of the consequences of her magic.

The lich unleashed another fireball, which missed David and slammed into the ground at Marie's feet. Heat rolled across my left leg. Marie's jacket smoldered, singed at the lapels and cuffs. The smoke became sharp with a plastic taint.

The bug at my neck moved, first along the front with skittish steps, then it paused, and diligently climbed the bottom of my chin, heading for my bottom lip.

THIRTEEN

I wanted to scream and frantically wished I could overcome Marie's compelling to do so, but that would open my mouth, and the bug was at my lips.

Marie had begun firing in rapid succession again, and her tail tore through the building, stabbing at the evasive lich. David darted deeper into the barn. Were I not compelled, I might have been able to help in some form. The Haven detection barely had the frozen witch alight, while the lich appeared lost in the darkness. The nearby flames helped obscure any last remnants of my spell.

I could sense disgust and panic at my plight, but my body did not shiver or flinch under Marie's magic. The crawling insects had found their way up my sleeves; most were between my jacket and shirt, and one terrifyingly determined bug worked around my button to my skin. One dallied about my right ankle, snagging in my sock. They might have been the centipedes David had been wearing, or something else. It truly didn't matter what kind they were, and I hoped I would never know. I had to lie and wait for Marie to stop the lich and remember me. Then again, I might die among the flames or get nibbled slowly by unidentified insects. The panic would have felt more real if my heartbeat raced or my breath quickened. Useless, I lay on my back, watching the rest of my team fight.

David, at least, moved unnaturally fast for being mangled by the draugr. I had no idea of the extent of his damage, but he appeared pretty lively. The faint glimmer of the lich glided smoothly, despite the onslaught of Marie's bullets and her dragon tail. David had stopped firing, perhaps out of ammunition or waiting for a sure shot as he had with the draugr.

The flames above me licked at the dry planks of the ceiling to my left. Some sections remained coated in gray mold and merely steamed from the heat. My entire world revolved around the burning building, Marie's back, and the torn hole in the far wall where the others battled. The smoke had thickened into a haze.

A particularly hellish scenario rolled through my mind where the lich once again made a run for it, Marie and David followed, and I hung on the floor of a burning barn as bug food. Even as the insect scurried along my bottom lip, I couldn't move. I had really hoped self-preservation would kick in at some point and overcome Marie's compelling.

The bug on my face crossed over my lips toward my nose.

My vision winked out as the lich let loose another Haven ball of light and I couldn't close my eyes. A fireball sounded as well, then two gunshots. My eyelids never blinked. I expected some of the sensations of panic, but my body refused my mind any satisfaction. Spots glittering in the darkness, I waited impotent, useless, and vulnerable. Shapes of the flames wavered in my dim vision.

One of the bugs fought against my shirt and the skin of my forearm. With one hesitant appendage, the worst tapped at the outer edge of my nostril.

"Cold sands," Marie swore in my comms. My ears echoed the gunshots, but I heard her and could only hope the lich was vanquished and we could restore me to some semblance of autonomy. Did she know what she'd done to me? "David? How bad?"

"I'm okay, Pyre." He sounded sluggish and his voice too slow. "I hate growing eyebrows."

"Kristen?"

I could see the dim shape of her movement in the smoke just beyond the broken wall. The burst of Haven light had been far enough away that it faded quickly. She stood close to where I remembered the witch had been. Any remnant of my Haven spell had faded.

The bug moved to my other nostril. Marie really needed to release me.

She stepped over the broken edge of a wall, studying me. "Crap." Her voice lowered and rang dully. "Released."

My heart exploded as I began with slapping at my face. I sucked in a shriek of a breath before ripping under my clothes with tendrils of Mer spells. "Shit. Shit!" I was stomping under the firelight with half a dozen lifting spells yanking bugs away from me. All the pent up panic made my chest feel like it might burst. Trapped and incapable of movement moments ago, I seemed unable to stop. I slapped the ground with a vengeful crushing spell before choking on the smoke. Embarrassed, I pulled a Haven detection spell last of all and glanced around the barn.

"The lich?" I asked. It didn't show in the white glows.

"I think David sent it back to Tarus." Marie stood close to the witch.

"After a bullet." David mumbled and I winced, wondering how damaged he was.

I had to unbutton my sleeve to get the last bug out. "Sorry, I was . . ." I didn't finish, not wanting to blame Marie. They'd done fine without me. I couldn't help but shiver and smooth over my jacket. The smoke thickened, and I moved away from the burning ceiling. The fight had been a nightmare. The feeling of impotence wrapped like a blanket over my earlier panic. "We should get out of here."

Marie shifted back toward the witch, appearing to ignore my comments. I was acting like a mad woman. Her tone full of compulsion, she addressed the man. "Where is Iliodor?"

Anger smoldered under a complacent tone. "I don't know."

The barn was quiet except for the crackling flames. Marie had certain questions she could compel. She wanted Iliodor to be involved, and I didn't think he was.

Her next question came with a tighter tone to her compulsion. "Who summoned the lich from Tarus?"

"I don't know." The hostility was in his tone, but a lilt toward the end made me believe the witch had just questioned the situation.

"Who—" Marie physically sagged. She likely intended to ask a question restrained by Consociation guidelines. I stepped closer as she gestured toward the man. "Bind him, Kristen."

I snapped a full binding around him, and he dropped heavily to the dirt. In his thirties, he wore a gray-blue hoodie and jeans. His chest seemed overly solid for his otherwise slight frame; perhaps he wore a vest like I did.

"Released." She studied me with a level of frustration.

The man stiffened visibly as he was freed from her spell and caught in mine. "Bring him."

I scoffed. He had to weigh over two hundred pounds. "I can't lift my own weight, let alone . . ." I faltered as her tail whipped out and wrapped around his legs.

Marie pointed toward the door behind me. "Move it. David?"

"On my way," he said from the back.

I scurried toward the opening, dodging around the clusters of bugs and broken boards left from the fight. The fire did not seem to be dwindling, but I assumed she had a plan. I cringed at the sound of the witch being dragged through the dirt.

"David, I need the Kuru out here. Tomas, send someone to the house and the barn after the Kuru are finished. I think we have a body in here as bait. I'll need a pickup for this witch." Marie's tone carried her usual gruffness and an anger which I rarely ever heard with her except for a brief exclamation.

I shivered as I stepped into the sunshine. The thought to check Haven passed, but I was getting tired. The amount of magic I'd used drained me. I still had to pee, but now I was thirsty. Turning after a few steps, I found Marie studying me with the witch being unceremoniously dragged over the threshold. Her tail released him, she tapped off her comms, and motioned me forward. I turned off my comms as I walked beside her to the edge of the field.

Her voice lowered, as if this conversation were just to be between us. "I'm sorry. That is one of the reasons we are not allowed to compel except for limited circumstances regarding Iliodor or Tarus."

"He would have crushed me." In reality, Marie could

have just shot the witch. She likely wanted to interrogate him about Iliodor.

"I made a mistake." She peered at me flatly, as if expecting a response.

I guessed she wouldn't want it mentioned. "Understood," I said. "It never happened. Why not David?" He hadn't seemed affected in the slightest, at least not by Marie's compulsion. "Or the lich?"

"Both are more resistant than normal humans and witches." She nodded, then her eyes flicked back toward the barn. Marie winced. "You're not good with illusion, right?"

As I glanced behind us to David, my jaw dropped before I could answer. He'd taken a heavy swipe across the right side of his face that had torn a flap of flesh from most of his cheek and jaw. It had bled down his face, neck, and shirt. The left side of his head had been seared with a fireball, and along with seared flesh, his hair had been burnt to the scalp above his ear.

David still managed a smile when I gaped at him. He had to hold his flapping skin to speak. "Got something in your hair."

I shook my curls, still feeling skeevy over the bugs. "Are you okay?"

"Wonderful." A centipede crawled out of his shirt.

I couldn't help but shiver and step back. "The lich?" I asked David.

"Pushed back into Tarus."

We still had the arcane user to find, the man in the red corvette. Marie dragged the immobile witch a few yards into the field, away from the smoking building. A distant siren sounded, causing me to glance back at the house. She tapped her comms back on, and so did I.

It was midday, and we'd tracked down the lich. The

trap with a witch and two draugrs had failed, and Marie had not gotten any closer to proving this was Iliodor.

"Who let the lich out?" David tried to speak in a singsong voice as he crouched down by the witch. "What's your name?"

I had to swap a new binding around the man to allow him to speak, and he fought against the less constrictive restraints. His expression gave no hint of being disturbed by David or any of us. Marie had exposed herself to him with compulsion and her tail. He gave no sense of being impressed and had no intention of responding to their interrogation.

Exhausted, I held his leash as they questioned him. I was still rattled from Marie's compelling and the bugs. The barn leaked smoke but appeared in no hurry to catch fire. The number of insects in the building was unnatural. Were they a byproduct of the lich or the arcane user? Tired and uncomfortable, I needed a moment to rest, focus, and see what I was missing.

A snapping crunch sounded from inside the barn, like a beam or support had just given up.

When the barn exploded, our captive smiled, or maybe it was a grimace.

CHAPTER
FOURTEEN

The blast shot through the roof of the building and sent the mass of destruction upward. The walls buckled, toppled, and folded in a dull roar. Birds shrieked and abandoned their cover in the surrounding brush and trees. Their calls and the rustle of dislodged leaves extended the clamor beyond the explosion.

Dirt and debris rolled toward us followed by the low whoosh of retreating pressure. Acrid smoke billowed above and seeped low along the ground. The expanding haze enveloped us.

I raised a shield, far too late. We would have been exposed if the explosion had been meant to reach us in the field. As chunks of metal roofing warbled down, I quickly shifted my spell to protect us against the raining wreckage. If we'd been inside, they might have even succeeded in eliminating Marie. "Bombs and snipers," I said while pulling out my phone to video the witch for Tomas to identify.

Marie tilted her head, studying me. "Yes. What about them?"

The air reeked, but I couldn't see fire in the ruins of the building. "Witches would have been focused on magical efforts to kill you. This has to be the arcane user, which meant they went through some effort to trap you here. What went wrong?"

David flicked a glance at me. "They missed?"

"Exactly. Why? What was the trigger?" We should have died in the building. I coughed from the acrid smoke. "Why not detonate the moment Marie entered?" It had been dark and impossible to identify any of us. They would have wanted to confirm she was inside. I pursed my lips and knelt by the witch.

Both his hands were clenched into fists, and his hoodie seemed bulky around the chest. His right thumb pressed against his index finger, exposing a black button attached to a device firmly in his grip. Was the witch compelled to kill Marie?

My pulse raced at the sight. I jumped away, shoved my phone in my pocket, and slammed a massive shield over his body. Marie and David couldn't see the realm magic, but my motion alerted them. I waved frantically. "Get back." My Dur-Alf shield flattened the side of the man's face and left an indent in the freshly tilled soil. My spell could hold back a fair-sized explosion, but at this proximity I couldn't be sure what force might leak around it. "I think he's wired with explosives. There's two dead man switches. He released the first when I swapped binding spells. He hadn't seen Marie before she . . ." I gestured toward the smoldering building. Marie's compulsion had saved us all inside the barn — which I wasn't supposed to talk about. How would we disarm the man?

David held his face with one hand and backed away, focused on the witch. "Explosives and snipers. We should be careful."

We'd cleared the lich, but the arcane user still remained. On top of that, we couldn't explain who had compelled the witches and other humans. Something was missing. We would have to be careful.

All three of us had been stepping deeper into the field. Holding the binding and shield from Dur-Alf on the witch, I plucked a detection spell from Haven and threw it back toward the ruined barn. I needn't have bothered. Two draugr were scrambling around the debris, one on each side. "Draugr."

The cryptids moved clumsily in the sunlight with their speed impeded as they clambered through broken wood. They couldn't get clear footing. We were twenty yards away from them, with the witch between us. The trap we'd been drawn into had been well planned.

"Crap." Marie stepped to my side and pulled my firearm. "I'm out, so is David. Bind 'em if you can."

My jaw slackened slightly as she took my weapon, but it did make sense. I had two spells going already, and if I lost those we might have a witch or an explosion to deal with. I tilted my head and frowned.

Marie caught my expression, then glanced back at the witch. "Do it. I hate to say it."

Feeling less than enthusiastic considering the witch had likely been compelled, I tugged a shield from Dur-Alf and put it between the witch and us. We had backed pretty far from the man when I let go of the shield covering him. I loosened his binding just the slightest bit.

The draugr were close to him when he detonated. Shrapnel embedded into the shield I'd placed between us. The cloud of dirt, explosives, and flesh hid the two draugr for a moment. When we could see their forms again, they were both sluggish and erratic, more so than they'd been earlier.

There might have been little we could do to disarm the bomb. Did the Consociation have a demolitions team? Probably. The bubble of guilt rose from my gut and floated in my chest. I'd let the compelled witch kill himself.

Marie stepped to the side; she could see my shield by the debris wedged into it. She took down one of the draugr with her first shot.

I stared at the dust and remains of the witch, flinching as she fired. Drained, I pulled a binding spell from Dur-Alf and spun it around my shield to the second draugr. It moved in unnaturally fast jerks, enough to dislodge my spell.

A bullet caved in the side of its head. Marie's next shot to the head dropped it.

Echoes of her shots died in the tilled field under the blue sky. The woods had gone silent. The birds and wildlife we'd disturbed had found someplace quiet to hide. The smoldering building and remains of the witch seethed with mute gray wisps.

I flinched when Marie handed me back my gun. Flushing, I dropped my shield and the shrapnel stuck in it. "Sorry." I swallowed quickly behind the words. Who was I apologizing to? A hollow pit hung in my chest.

"It's not easy when innocents die." Marie barely glanced at me. "We need to end this. Any leads, Tomas? Otherwise, we need to get David looked at, then we hit up the sniper's apartment."

Shoving down my guilt, I focused on David's wounds. He'd taken the worst damage of the three of us, and I expected him to be complaining about the condition of his suit.

"Some gauze, and I'll be okay, Pyre." He pointed back toward the house where the trap had started. "I'd feel a little better with some ammo, truthfully."

Marie waved off David's comment. "ETAs, Tomas? Sorry we've got you covering all this."

Finn coughed. "Pyre, he's got me up to speed, and I've been monitoring since about the first explosion. I've got Kuru on site, and they're alerted to possible traps."

I glanced back at the house, expecting to see the taco truck parked out front.

"I can have a simple medic there in just over fifteen, Pyre." Tomas's tone was slightly apologetic. "The closest healer is with Finn at the moment."

"Simple medic to evaluate." Marie peered at the smoking ruins and nudged her head back toward the house before leading us away. "We've got three draugr bodies out here along with two witches in the rubble and worse. The locals had to have heard the explosions, and even if you kept them from the emergency calls, they'll be nosing around."

"I've got the local FBI arriving in seven minutes, Pyre. They are at six agents now and five more within an hour. They had live comms so there is an obvious concern about the situation. Should I tell them to coordinate with you at the scene?"

Marie grumbled to herself before answering. "Yes. I'll make it quick. They aren't going to like it that we'll be taking the FBI bodies." All three of us kept checking around us, as if expecting more draugr to come traipsing out of the woods. "Where are you on the sniper's burner phone and ammo? Specialized ammo doesn't come easily."

"Reg Simpson connected with four phones from the burner, all of which were used in a wide rural area north of your location. I've tried pinging, but they're turned off." Tomas's voice shifted and keys clacked. "I'm tracking the ammo from the assassination scene by component properties, which means I'm using Udy's help. He's got the analysis started. There are a lot of people who make specialized ammo, especially in or around the Carolinas."

I would be interested in seeing Reg's apartment. "Tomas, does Reg Simpson have a job?"

"Occasional work as security at events."

"Anything unusual in his attendance over the past week?" I was careful when digging for information with Tomas, as sometimes he took my questions badly.

"No set schedule nor missing shifts. He doesn't have a personal routine from what I could backtrack. The best I could trace from phone activity is in an email I sent an hour ago."

I grimaced. We were almost to the house at the front of the property. Perhaps I'd have a minute to go through the emails while we waited.

David was understandably quiet, and Marie appeared to be brooding. We had too many unfinished leads and even more questions. I walked through what we knew, focused on the conference center room before the assassination with the lich and zombie Jenny being let inside. The guard, Bill, would have the best access to disable the cameras, but did he have the technical know-how?

"Tomas, would Bill Jackson have the expertise to disable the cameras on his own?"

"Not from what I see in his education and experience, but anyone could follow instructions to place the devices."

The arcane user might have a technical background, or there was another player we hadn't found yet. "Is there anything unusual about the equipment that might give us a lead?"

"I didn't see anything, but the report is in your email."

Though Tomas couldn't see, I smiled apologetically and pulled out my phone as we walked through the last few steps of the field. The closest FBI agent's mangled body had attracted a few flies.

Suzanne, since she drove zombie Jenny to the conference center, might have also let the lich inside. The cryptid's ability to become invisible could have allowed it to be there at any point prior to Marie's arrival; it could have entered with Bill or through an open loading dock. When had it been summoned? Before the assassination, I knew most of Suzanne's and Jenny's timelines. The guard's schedule had been limited to work and his apartment. All three lived alone. Perhaps the suicide bomber witch would give us a lead.

"Tomas, any identification on the video I sent you?"

He swore. "I would have let you know."

Of course he would. I frowned at myself for not thinking it through. I'd felt so helpless in the last attack that I was pushing to be of some use. Marie's dour mood wasn't due to my actions, but I couldn't help feeling like the weak link in the team.

It had been just over twenty-four hours since the first attempted attack on Marie. I glanced back at the smoldering ruins at the edge of the fields. Had all this been planned since that failed attempt to kill her at the conference center? Gathering the explosives would prove the most difficult. The arcane user could have easily summoned the four draugr, though I couldn't see how they could be compelled to act in staged concert. It certainly wasn't in their nature.

We walked around the house on the opposite side of the garage. If the Kuru were around, I saw no sign of them.

"We'll want the explosives analyzed. Of everything here, they would have been the hardest to acquire in a short time frame. Maybe in their haste, someone left a trail."

Finn came back on the comms. "I'll have the Kuru retain samples and bring them back to the archives for Udy to analyze. I'll jump onto Discord and let them know. Finding an emoji for explosion shouldn't be hard."

I frowned at Finn's comment, but I'd never asked about his contact with the Kuru. I'd just assumed that he was texting them.

We circled to the front of the building where I could make out the third agent's body. Three of the FBI had died in this attempt to trap Marie, along with two civilians, and I'd let the witch commit suicide. In all my cases with the DRC so far, this one had the most casualties.

"We're headed to the sniper's apartment after this?" I asked Marie. After feeling so useless in the barn, I needed to move forward in some way.

She studied me. "We are. You okay?"

A bug crawled out of David's sleeve and I shivered. "Not really," I answered.

CHAPTER
FIFTEEN

While Marie dealt with the local FBI, I sat in the Hummer catty-corner behind David. Tomas had sent us a dozen reports since morning, but none gave me any sense of a clear lead. The search for a red corvette in the Winston-Salem area had gone nowhere. I asked Tomas to cross-reference *any* registered owners of such vehicles in North Carolina with our Consociation database, and he'd grudgingly obliged with no results. The chemical analysis of the ammo appeared promising with specific chemicals identified, but that had just come in. The phone logs of the sniper's burner phone had two unidentified numbers called repeatedly over the past five days.

A siren sounded behind us, and I twisted in my seat to peer down the dirt drive. The newest FBI vehicles were clustered there, as Marie didn't want them near the house or their fallen teammates. She just needed them to keep the locals away until the Consociation and Kuru could clean up.

"Your medic is on site," Tomas said sharply.

David nodded. He wasn't his usual self. He didn't act like he was in pain, but I knew he could control it. As he opened his door, a breeze pushed his slightly putrid scent to the back. His clothes added the smell of burnt polyester.

I slipped my phone in my pocket and exited. "I'll go with you, David."

An emergency vehicle with flashing lights bounced down the rutted road that served as the house's drive. Two black SUVs nearly blocked the entrance. The agents hadn't gotten far from their vehicles. The woman glaring at Marie had on an FBI windbreaker rather than a suit. Her eyes were sharp and angry. The three men with her appeared hostile as well.

Marie's comms were off, so I focused on the conversation as we passed behind them. She had the smooth but firm tone she used when dealing with other departments. "It's going to take us a while to make sure we've cleared all the traps. I've got specialists coming in to handle everything. I don't want to risk anyone else."

In the distant field, the smoke from the blasted barn had disappeared. Finn had promised the Kuru would make sure a fire couldn't start.

The FBI woman squinted at me and David before gesturing toward the house. "Those are *my* people. *I'm* responsible for their bodies."

"You will get them. We need to clear them first. Forty-eight hours. I can understand how important it is to retrieve their bodies. I would feel the same way." Marie's patient tone belied her previous stress. We all wanted to follow up on the leads. David had sent the lich back into Tarus, but whoever had summoned it could do so again if we didn't stop them.

The woman's voice emphasized her part in the slaughter. "*I* assigned them to this property. *I'm* the one who has to explain this to their families." The FBI agent frowned as we crossed behind their vehicles; perhaps she'd seen David's face.

"Their families will want their bodies. They will get them. It will be two days, though." Marie repeated her previous arguments firmly.

The emergency vehicle pulled up behind the FBI's SUVs, and a familiar woman jumped out of the driver's side. An athletic frame with short black hair, she wore the same EMT uniform she had when she'd helped with Finn. Her expression never wavered when she saw David's face. Holding his skin in place, he smiled at her.

Finn spoke over the comms. "We've got another body in the barn, burned in the blast like the one they dragged from the house."

The bloody trail we'd followed across the field had been either father or son from the residence, we'd assumed, since the Kuru only confirmed that a single body had been left in the house. The only reason I could imagine the witch or draugr moving the corpse would be to lead us into the field.

"Any chance of identification?" I asked.

"Maybe with Herta's help."

The attendant opened the back door to the emergency vehicle and motioned David inside. I recognized Dowlin's voice. "Well, that's a mess. You know I can't do much with your ilk, right?"

I peered inside as David climbed in. Gratefully, Dowlin hadn't attempted a human illusion. "Because he's a vampire?" I asked.

"An abomination, whatever you call it." Dowlin motioned for David to lie on the gurney. "The cells are half-twisted with Tarus contamination. Humans shouldn't be messing with that realm. Any other race knows that."

David didn't argue, and I couldn't see his expression. I had nothing to say in defense. Becoming a vampire was usually a voluntary action which required at least grasping the realm, if not pulling yourself partially into it. I'd never questioned David about his situation or choices. There had been accidental infections. Few had firmly grasped the Tarus realm intentionally for more than a moment and not been affected, much like Ya Keya and werewolves, though exceptions existed.

Dowlin gestured to the woman in the EMT uniform. "I'll need some gauze and tape. Best I can do is coax the human part of the flesh to attach. He'll have to finish it on his own."

I startled when Marie spoke sharply from beside me. "How long will you need?" Her eyebrows had been singed, and her clothes stunk of smoke.

"Give me fifteen minutes, Anka." Dowlin tilted his head and brushed his chin with the back of his index finger in what seemed some odd sign of respect.

When we were alone, I could ask Finn what 'Anka' meant. I turned to Marie. "Finn says the Kuru found a second body inside the barn. Burned."

Marie tapped on her comms. "Tomas, tell Herta I need identifications a priority. How soon can we get her the bodies?"

"This afternoon, Pyre. Transports are almost there, and I'm finalizing logistics since the body count has gone up."

It was midday already with the sun high in a blue sky. Tomas must plan on flying the bodies back to Atlanta if he expected them to be there in a few hours. A distant helicopter thudded in the distance, but I couldn't see it. The urge to pee had become insistent.

"What do you have?" Marie asked.

Focused on my bladder and the dwarf healing a vampire, she caught me off guard, and I flustered at the comment. "Well, the lich is dead — rather, expelled back to Tarus."

Marie's face shone in some areas, as if newly healed skin covered her left cheek and forehead. "And . . ."

I drew in a deep breath, focusing. "The source of the ammo and the records of the cell phone would still be useful. The red corvette owner is yet to give us a lead. The identities of the suicide witch and the other body might lead us somewhere, but we have no idea yet." Ticking off the items gave me a moment to realize she wanted my assessment of our next course of action. Unless the arcane user popped up and gave us a lead, we'd have to dig in where we could. "We glove up and search the house while David is being worked on."

Marie tilted her head. "But . . ."

"We head to the sniper's apartment if we don't find a lead."

CHAPTER

SIXTEEN

Shoes wrapped in plastic, I stood at the edge of the kitchen, videoing the scene for Tomas. Marie would let the regular FBI inside once the body had been retrieved by our people. Based on a section of a forearm I found by the stove, I believed we had the father, Terrence Flowers, here in the kitchen.

Marie called down the hall from the back. "The draugr, and maybe the witch, entered through the screened-in porch. I'm guessing the door was not opened by draugr. The attack starts here and works toward the kitchen. Any luck on the suicide bomber's identification?"

I frowned when Tomas did not chastise Marie as he had me. "Nothing yet, Pyre."

"I wish we had a forensic kit here for the entry."

Finn cleared his throat and came onto the comms. "Pyre, Leah is almost done with her flagged reviews. She has nothing significant from them and needs an hour to get reports done. Would you rather I send her there with a kit? We could have an ID in a couple hours."

"That's good, Finn. Let's get that working."

I had rudimentary knowledge, but wouldn't have wanted to risk pulling the prints myself. Perhaps, considering the type of unit we were, I should learn, as Leah had.

"Kristen, lets meet back at the Hummer. David, you patched up?"

His voice was muffled and unintelligible.

"Whatever. We'll be right out. Heading to the sniper's apartment. Tomas, where's my transports?"

"The first two are a quarter mile from the turn into the residence, Pyre."

I sent Tomas a last video of the ceiling, turned for the front door, and considered sneaking into the victim's bathroom, but knew better. The cluster of FBI agents had grown, and a third vehicle nearly blocked the Hummer where David waited in his passenger seat. The emergency vehicle had left.

Marie snapped off booties and gloves as she marched from the back. She noted the growing crowd of FBI but didn't react.

We passed as she opened the driver's door. I grimaced. "I'm going to need a quick stop before we get back on the road."

"Understood."

As I climbed in, I got a good look at David. I assumed it was him, under the gauze. Most of the layers wrapped from the top of his head around his ears and under his jaw, but Dowlin had managed a couple laps across the chin and under the nose, almost covering his lips. "Looks like doc was on a roll," I said.

David spoke, barely moving his lips. "I don't think he liked my face. However . . ." He lifted a bag of blood with the tube cut short and tucked it between the gauze like a straw.

I barely shivered at the sight, and as Marie glanced in

the mirror, I twisted to peer behind us. Two yellow box trucks were rumbling down the drive. "Finn, do I need to give them any details?" she asked.

"No, Pyre. You already briefed us earlier. Tomas and I mapped out what we could from the transponder and audio."

As the two trucks pulled past, Marie dug into the dirt and launched the Hummer past the FBI. Despite her driving, I was invested in finding a bathroom and stared out the windshield. A pair of small vehicles raced toward us, kicking dust into the air. As we neared, the two kids riding ATVs jumped off the road and booked into the woods. The hazy cloud cleared as Marie raced through the leafless forest.

A white pickup was parked at the corner of the resident's drive and the rural highway. A shirtless man with a sandy-colored mullet pounded on the closed side panel of the Kuru's taco truck. The woman with him peered through the front windows at the steering wheel.

David pointed to the left and slurped the last of his blood bag as we launched past the locals. Marie took the turn without slowing.

Pulling out my cell phone, I busied myself with Reg Simpson's location. It would take us nearly an hour of backtracking toward Winston-Salem to get to his apartment north of the city. I'd have time to catch up on reports. I was tired and sore from the skirmish, but in much better shape than my teammates. Curling up on the floor while they fought hadn't taken that much out of me.

After using the gas station's facilities, I grabbed a small coffee and pocketed creamer and sugar. The only reason I considered taking the time was because Marie was filling a cup when I came out. Until the tight-lipped young girl behind the glass kept glancing nervously from us to her register, I hadn't considered how rough we might appear.

Her pale skin blanched when David entered with his head nearly covered in gauze. He strode directly to the sunglass rack and picked up a dark black pair.

Marie sighed as she approached the counter jabbing a thumb at me and nodding her head toward David. "On my card."

He strode up behind Marie with his face nearly covered in bandages and dark tinted glasses. I could see the smile he wore as he pointed to a cheap fedora on a shelf behind the counter.

We had a long ride ahead, so I dug deep on the sniper's background. "Reg Simpson is out of Jacksonville. He lived on the block opposite Jojo's Nightclub and moved out of his apartment fourteen days after the deaths at the rave."

Marie turned up to her mirror. "You think there's a connection?"

"I've never seen his name in the cold case file." It bothered me that there might be a connection.

Tomas spoke over the comms, and his high pitch sounded almost jeering. "Almost thirty percent of the residents moved within sixty days of the massacre. Fifty percent of the nearby employees left their jobs in a two-block radius. I see no other connection to Reg Simpson and any victim or employee of the rave, which is why his name is not in the cold case file."

Reg Simpson's life had been a bit sketchy at points after he'd come back from the middle east. He had an honorable discharge and medical notes for PTSD, which appeared to lead to a few rough years. But two years before the rave, he'd settled into a stable routine, and it continued even after he left Jacksonville. I doubted he worked as a sniper of his own accord.

His phone records led nowhere, not even family, just work. The only difference in mine would have been the calls to Jade. I'd made the choice to allow my career and distance come between us.

I would call her tonight. Jade had followed her father's advice and avoided the covens and witches who might be able to guide her in dealing with her powers. Someday, I hoped she would get help. I sometimes felt the coward who ran from her problem toward my job.

We pulled between a pair of single-story apartment buildings with three scrawny dogs barking while they skittered toward the back corner. Marie left the Hummer running. "Stay here, David. You look ridiculous."

He was working on his fourth blood bag and silently turned toward her. Only his ears and lips showed now that he wore the dark glasses and fedora.

The dogs continued to bark and whine until Marie spoke quietly. "Stow it." All three sat, then rested on their elbows, attentive and silent.

Crime scene tape marked the door. When I cleared our way into Reg Simpson's apartment, I knew the local police had already investigated, yet I didn't trust that the arcane user hadn't returned to set a trap for us.

I hoped we might gain another lead from the Flowers' residence, or at least from the video I took before I'd let the bomber kill himself. The situation at the barn bothered me the most from this case. I should have been more rattled by the minotaur who hurt Finn, but it was my own inability, caused by Marie, which ate at me. Along with that came a deeper shame in letting the witch commit suicide. I still couldn't see a clearer path around the situation, but I kept revisiting it.

Reg Simpson had been a neat man. The kitchen counter had an empty dish drain beside the sink. The coffee pot had a matching set of brown and red jars beside it. The small dining table had two seats with salt and pepper beside the napkin stand. The appliances, floor, and walls were old, but clean.

I'd lit my detection from Haven and could make out the glows of the neighbors in the apartment to our right. Reg's bathroom had a little more clutter on the counter, but neatly stowed and cleaner than most men's.

Marie waited in the center of the kitchen as I tugged at Dur-Alf and opened the pantry. I did not see a sign that the police had searched anywhere until we got to the bedroom.

Reg Simpson had startled local police into shooting him as he brandished a pistol. Any evidence of weapons had been removed from the room, and that included the odd ammo Tomas had retrieved and had Udy analyzing. The disarray of the bed, desk, and closets appeared to be from the police, based on the status of the rest of the apartment. They were investigating a deranged veteran, not a sniper. We hadn't learned about their search until after the fact, and we hadn't given them anything further to worry about.

"Not one personal picture." Marie pointed to the walls and desk. "They took his laptop." A mouse and wires pointed to the empty place. "Tomas, see if you can locate Reg's laptop."

"It's not in the inventory, Pyre. I'll send a request."

With gloved hands, I pulled out a small, torn cardboard box from under the desk. "Packaging?" The wire trash basket had other debris, but this had been tossed haphazardly out of the way. I flattened it to expose the hand-written packing slip.

"Addressed to R. Simpson." Marie flipped an edge to expose the rest of the package. "This wasn't mailed."

The label had been attached to a plain cardboard box, but never stamped or sent through the post office. I noticed an overlap and pulled a lifting spell from Mer. Stickers worked easier with magic; I could create a very precise edge, especially since our hands were gloved. It took a moment to expose a printed shipping label. "We might have just found the manufacturer. Benjamin Poore out of Madison, NC." I snapped a picture of the address and sent it to Tomas. "Should I look it up and call?"

Marie nodded, sniffing the packaging. "Before it gets too late. Hopefully someone other than the sniper paid for it or ordered it."

I hoped the same. There had been an intention to mail the ammo, then a new label had been slapped on, so someone hadn't wanted that trail. My pulse rose, and my cheeks flushed with excitement. We hadn't had a decent lead yet, and this appeared to be a mistake we weren't supposed to find.

The phone rang as I waited and prodded at the packaging. It had been torn open and discarded in a rough, sloppy manner which didn't fit with the rest of Reg's behaviors. My call went to voicemail. "Poore's Bait and Ammo. Leave a message." The man's voice had a heavy country drawl. I hung up.

Tomas spoke. "Just sent you what I know of the company and owner, Pyre. Benjamin Poore, age 53. He's owned the business for twelve years. No immediate flags with the Consociation database. Seth Monroe is the only employee at the store and a friend. No connections or flags there either."

"Personal cell phone?" Marie asked.

My phone dinged with a text. "Sent to your phones, Pyre. I've already emailed it in the preliminary report." Tomas added the latter comment with usual snark.

Marie gestured for me to call the number and I did. There was little left in the bedroom to dig through, as it had been already exposed from the previous search. I doubted we'd find much in the bathroom or kitchen cabinets. The call ended after two rings, and a message informed me that no voice mail had been set up. Without waiting for Marie's prompt, I called the number again on speaker while I dug up Tomas's most recent email, which I assumed had an address for Benjamin's residence. I had no doubt we'd be heading there.

My number had been blocked. Marie frowned. "Address."

"I'm pulling it up now," I said. "He's in Ellisboro."

"He's at his sister's house. Agnes Poore. I'll text the address."

My lip tugged to one side. "How do you know?"

Marie smiled and motioned me toward the door.

Tomas swore. "I tracked his cell because it wasn't bouncing through towers near his residence. His sister lives in Dillard, NC, near where his phone is answering."

I followed Marie through Reg's neat living room and kitchen to the front door. "Finn, send local FBI over here to get prints off the packaging we left and comb the apartment."

"Got it, Pyre." Finn responded quickly with an almost cheery response. I understood the sense of being left out and searching for an opportunity to be of use.

The three dogs watched us from the back of the property. Across the parking lot in front of the opposite set of apartments, a pot-bellied man in a too-tight t-shirt sat in a dark green camping chair, smoking something. He studied us without a particular interest or expression.

"Marie. Someone still compelled Reg to take his sniper shots. I'd like to see if his neighbor noticed anything." We should really interview neighbors of anyone who had been suspiciously influenced. Unless the arcane user had a unique talisman or special rituals, we were searching for someone who could compel. That list was very short; demon, jinn, and dragon-shifter.

She gestured for me to lead the way. The heavyset man had a stubble from two or three days of not shaving, greasy brown hair, and a tan line around his neck.

"Feds?" he asked as we approached. He smoked a tiny cigar, and the tobacco barely covered the undertones of marijuana.

"Yes, FBI." I showed him my badge, then gestured across the parking lot to Reg's residence. "Do you know the neighbor in that apartment?"

"Sarge, we call him. Ex-military and a stickler for dumpster regulations. The police were out here, but they wouldn't say nothing." He cocked his head and smirked. "What he do?"

"Before the police came out, did you notice Sarge having any visitors?"

The man laughed, drew in a hit, and made us wait before he answered through a hazy breath. "Never a one. He's a loner."

Marie sighed. "Are you here all the time?"

"Yep. Disabled. Damn, what have you been up to, woman?" He pointed at his eyebrows.

She ignored him and nodded me back toward the Hummer. "We'll come back through and get proper inter-views later."

I agreed and flashed the man a quick smile. "Thank you."

David pointed at the dogs when we got back into the vehicle. "How do you do that, Pyre?" He appeared to have finished his blood bags, but his voice was still muffled from the excessive bandages.

She buckled into her seat. "Do you have the address up?" she asked him.

"Yeah."

The Hummer jerked as she punched us backward into a tight circle and came to a stop with us aimed out of the parking lot. "Left or right, David?"

I grabbed my last water out of my go bag and slid down in the back seat to read Tomas's reports. The trip would be easier if I didn't watch the road.

The information on Benjamin wasn't helpful, and I backtracked through some of Leah's interviews with the employees of the conference center to see if anything stuck out. Later questions had revolved around trying to lock in on Suzanne and Bill's activities and when they might have sabotaged the video equipment or brought in the lich or zombie Jenny.

The more I mulled on the compelling, I began to wonder if the elusive arcane user might be the key. I spoke over the comms, knowing everyone could hear and might join in. "Finn, I've heard of old grimoires mentioning rituals designed to control jinn or demons with a binding or cage. No one really believed it in my circles. However, superstition and myth are often based on fact. Do you know of anything like that?"

"Those have been purged," Marie said.

I straightened, risking a view of the front window to glance into the mirror to gauge her expression. "So, it is possible."

"Unfortunately. If we could have captured the lich instead of banishing it, I would have searched its body for proof."

"Is that why you believe Iliodor is involved? Does he

know of this?" I didn't ask what she might consider evidence of these rituals.

"He's too young to know firsthand, but if anyone could dig this up, it would be Iliodor." Marie's tone dripped with bitterness at the mention of his name. She wanted to blame him, but I couldn't see him using Tarus in this way.

There was little point in revisiting the argument. "If this is not a restrained jinn or demon, is a dragon-shifter a possibility?" I knew little of their race or politics, but Marie's own daughter was on Earth.

"No." Her tone had no malice or resentment, just a solid belief that her people were not involved. "Tomas, do you have a number for the sister?"

"I've got it," I said perhaps a little too proudly. I'd copied it off one of his reports in case we needed it. Benjamin had blocked me, but the sister might not.

"Save it for when we're at the house." Marie didn't appear impressed, but maybe Tomas appreciated someone reading his reports in a timely manner. Her tone remained brusque and intense. "I hope we haven't spooked him already. David, how much longer? Ten minutes?"

"Over twenty."

"Crap." She swerved into a side road next to a gas station we had been passing. The driver of a Prius waiting to turn at the stop sign pulled back from her window as the front bumper skimmed by her. "They could have filled it up."

I didn't mind the opportunity for a quick stop and ended up with passable cup of coffee for the ride north in rural North Carolina. We only had one close call with a logging truck pulling out in front of Marie, and I managed not to spill a drop.

"Time?" Marie asked.

"Eight and a half, Pyre. It'll be on the right." He still sounded muted.

My pulse rose at the countdown, and I finished my coffee. This didn't seem likely to be a trap; the clues were too tenuous. Whoever orchestrated this attack on Marie would have had to count on us finding the ammo packaging and the hidden mailing address, then tracking Benjamin to his sister's, but I'd still be wary.

Benjamin's sister lived in a double-wide in a clearing on a five-acre property of sparse pine. I could make out his beat-up Chevy truck parked at the side of the house as we turned into the drive. I assumed the faded blue Toyota Corolla belonged to his sister, Agnes. A flimsy wire trailer held a cream-colored washer and dryer that had yellowed with age. The neighboring lands were wild woods of mostly leafless oaks. After our last surprise with the draugr, I'd check the boundaries with Haven. The thought of pulling more magic from the realms exhausted me.

Marie stopped a good distance from the residence. "David, stay here."

"Afraid I'll scare them?"

"Yes, but I'm enjoying the muzzle." Marie had her door open before I'd released my buckle.

I jumped out as she waited for me at the front of the Hummer. The engine smelled hot. The fragrant pines around us settled my nerves as I pulled into Haven.

The front door of the house opened to expose a thin, short man with a green cap. I guessed Benjamin based on his height and weight in the report. The shotgun he held aimed at the ground rested from his shoulder to ankle.

"Private property." His tone was not threatening. He stepped out of the doorway as he spoke, closing the door behind him. I appreciated that he didn't want his sister involved.

I flicked a detection spell to the left, and it picked up Benjamin with a hazy glow along with some small animals and birds. Marie held up her badge while I tugged at Dur-Alf. I doubted anything too close to the house would show. We were fifteen paces away.

"FBI. Special Agent Marie Pyre. We're here to discuss some of your work. You're going to have to put that weapon away."

Despite my earlier confidence, my chest tightened as I felt both trapped and exposed in the man's front yard. I studied the windows of the house while I tossed a second detection spell to our right. We'd have a bit of warning if some draugr decided to climb out of the dried underbrush. Still, I flicked glances into the surrounding woods.

Benjamin nodded and slid his grip off the trigger and onto the barrel before raising the weapon and moving back toward the house. "This about Seth?"

Marie waited until he leaned the weapon against the building and Benjamin started to return to us before she spoke. "What happened to Seth?"

Benjamin glanced at his feet as he walked. "Don't know. I sent him to deliver the ammo because my sister needed me to pick up a washer and dryer that her friend from the church wanted to get rid of. I was happy to have Seth go. The guy gave me the creeps. Anyway, Seth up and disappears. I got a bad feeling and just holed up here for a day or two." His face slightly flushed, I guessed he felt guilty over his employee. "It went bad, didn't it?"

Finn spoke quietly over the comms. "I'll call Seth Monroe's phone and check in with his wife if he doesn't answer."

Marie offered a sad smile for the sagging man in front of us. "Might be. Why don't you take us through this from the beginning? Who is this guy and when did he approach you?"

Benjamin dug at his ear. "I don't know his name, but he had me call him Fade. Stops by the shop about ten days ago, maybe two weeks. Says he wants some special ammo." I started at the time frame. How long had this been planned?

"Can you describe him?" Marie asked.

"City folk with polished shoes and a weird hat. Probably lives in a big property out in the country but never steps in the grass. That kind of people. He stares at you like he wants to pull something out of you. Who calls themselves Fade?" Benjamin shivered.

"Special ammo," Marie prompted.

"Really weird. I've got the list at the shop. He gives me ten grand in hundreds, the list, and the phone. Tells me to call when I've got it ready." Benjamin twitched. "I never should have taken the money."

"Do you have the number you called?"

"Only contact in the phone. Under Fade. Seth has — had the phone."

"When did you call this Fade?"

"Three days ago in the morning. I figure he's going to come by and get it. He tells me to wait for a call and then deliver the ammo. It was that evening some guy calls and says to mail it to him."

"Not Fade?"

"No. Reg Simpson. I just finish printing a mailing label and Fade calls saying I got to deliver it that afternoon, but I already promised Agnes. So, I sent Seth."

"To Reg Simpson's address?"

"Yes."

I wilted at Benjamin's response. We had no real name for the red corvette man, no new description, and no location. There might be fingerprints on the list he provided or on the money.

"You covered your mailing label?" Marie asked.

Benjamin closed his eyes and bit his lip. "I knew this was trouble. I should have told Seth to run when he called me."

"He called you after he went out to deliver the package?"

"Yeah. Fade changed the meetup location. Closer to Seth, so he don't mind. He still let me know, though."

A smile fluttered across my lips. "Where did he move the delivery to?" I asked. We might have an actual lead.

CHAPTER

SEVENTEEN

I waited as Benjamin wilted further and sighed. "Virginia. Martinsville. It's just over the state line. I really didn't think there'd be any trouble. I've known Seth most of my life."

Marie tapped her chin. "How quickly can you and your sister get out of the house?"

Benjamin blanched, and his lips worked silently before he spoke. "She won't leave her cats."

"We'll provide a house where she can bring them. I'm hoping only a day or two. This Fade is very dangerous and does not leave witnesses."

"Seth?"

I winced at the pain in his question, and Marie drew a deep breath. "You should leave now." She turned toward me, but spoke to Tomas. "Can we get an FBI escort out here? How quickly?"

Tomas swore. "Let me check, Pyre."

"I need to talk to Agnes." His eyebrows raised as if he didn't relish the idea.

Marie nudged her chin toward the building. "Go, but

make it quick. I'll wait here for your answer, but it should be yes."

His eyes squinted and he nodded his head quickly before turning for the building.

I had not expected her to pause even a minute before heading to Virginia. We could be driving hours or another fifteen minutes, but Marie would head there even without an exact location. I watched her as Benjamin walked, then jogged toward the house, veering to grab his shot gun.

I leaned toward her. "We're going to check it out, right?"

She tilted her head with a slight roll of her eyes. "Tomas, what do you have for me?"

"Red corvette owner, Dahlia Roberts, residing outside the city of Martinsville, VA, Pyre. I've texted David the coordinates. No activity on phone records for the past five days. An elderly white woman widowed last year who appears to live by herself on a twenty-acre estate."

Marie grumbled. "I'm going to assume she's dead, or compelled. We have to hope the arcane user is still at her residence. What's my travel time?"

"Forty-six minutes, Pyre. Do you want me to divert Leah as backup? She'd be at least thirty minutes behind you."

"No. I'm going to hope he's not expecting us. He didn't leave us these breadcrumbs."

"FBI at your location in twenty, Pyre."

"I'm not waiting. Get me local enforcement to park at the street. If Benjamin hasn't been located so far, we should be fine. I'll know in a minute what his time frame is. Do you have a safe house for me?"

"Yes, Pyre."

"Then we'll be heading momentarily to Virginia." She

studied me. "Any connections in our database to the owner of the corvette?"

"No arcane interests, Pyre. She's a devout Baptist."

Benjamin hopped out of the house and ran toward us. His jaw set tight, he blinked too frequently, and was breathing heavily when he reached us. "We'll be out of here in five minutes. She's pissed."

Marie relaxed. "Tomas, text the sister the address and reroute FBI to the location. Forget local." She forced a smile for Benjamin. "Make it quick. The agents will be at the site we're relocating you to. They can provide anything you need. I'm hoping we'll clear this up today."

"And Seth?"

"We'll let you know what we find." She pointed him back toward his house and led the way back to the Hummer.

"I've got no records of a body, Pyre. No local disturbances. Do you want a BOLO on Seth's car?"

"Yes, thank you, Tomas."

I sprinted for my door, glancing at David who leaned an elbow against his window, bandaged cheek tilted into his palm. The feeling of being left out of an investigation I understood. He'd have his chance when we got to the unfortunate widow's estate. From what I'd seen of this case so far, I doubted we'd find her alive, or Seth for that matter. We could hope that the arcane user did not expect to find us, but I wasn't willing to dismiss there being a trap.

While Marie raced off the property and followed David's directions, I dug into my emails, sure that Tomas would have sent us information. Surprisingly, Finn had emailed pictures and a map of the two-story residence from a real estate listing. The bottom floor had a spacious layout connected to a garage while the upstairs held eight rooms including baths.

From the images, we'd be visible nearly a quarter mile from the road to the estate along a paved driveway surrounded by open lawn. I pulled up an image of the property. The only cover near the house was a small barn and paddock on the east side where the attached garage blocked visibility from the ground floor.

"I think we should park the Hummer at the neighbor's and cut through the woods at the east side on foot. If he's watching the front drive, we'll be easy to spot. We might have a chance to reach the house without being seen if we sneak up."

Marie peered up at me through the mirror. "The less time we give him to prepare the better. Let's hope he's alone. Send David the neighbor's address. Tomas, I want a small team of local FBI agents to arrive five minutes after we do and cordon off the street and driveway. They are not to approach."

David rattled his mints and pressed one between his lips. He glanced back at me with his sunglasses. I could sense his smile.

Tomas took a moment to respond. "Sorry, Pyre. I'm waiting on Stacey for contact with the local FBI. She jumped in when I acquired the safe house and sent two agents."

"Dancing monkeys. Keep me updated." Marie raced around a slower car ahead, and I slunk down to send David the new address and check my emails again as car horns sounded.

Surprisingly fast, Herta had identified the witch at the barn as a man out of Boston. I groaned inwardly when I saw Tomas's reply indicating the direct connection to Iliodor. He was a radical follower who had been involved in two incidents involving the Consociation. I had no intention of alerting Marie yet.

Twenty minutes later, Herta confirmed the son as one of the bodies while the last body in the barn belonged to a forty-three-year-old Tennessee resident and mercenary with legal entanglements involving arson and explosives. At least neither of them had any Consociation records. As we drove the last five minutes down a rural highway, I focused on the map, trying to decide if we should come in through the garage door and laundry room or the back patio.

Tomas spoke as we drove past the first house in a neighborhood of elegant estates. "The occupants have agreed to stay inside the house when you arrive. They aren't pleased." I could make out the roof of Dahlia Roberts' house through the trees.

When we drove onto the neighbor's property, Marie parked along the west edge of the drive. A man scowled from a downstairs window but remained inside. "Move it. Kristen, you lead. You want to stick with your entry point?" She'd deferred to my assessment, despite how uncomfortable it made me.

I scrambled out the door, seat belt already unbuckled. "Garage, then laundry. It means two doors, but it might give us the best detection with Haven before we breech. I'm expecting wards, but I can only find Dur-Alf or Mer. The patio entrance has too many windows." I wasn't about to tug on Tarus or Ya Keya.

The only contingency we couldn't circumvent was another exploding building, so I was to remain at the rear of the team while David and Marie rushed in. I fought the nagging lie that whispered I was unfit for the job; I'd proven myself a number of times.

She grunted an assent and gestured for me to cross the lawn toward the copse of pine and oak that separated the properties. David cocked his head at me, still trying for a reaction to his fedora-covered gauze. The sun hung low over our target, forcing me to squint. The scent of the past night's rain and new growth rose from the ground as we ran.

I frowned at the black metal fence dividing the properties. It hadn't shown in the images. "Crap."

"I can clear that," David said.

Marie grumbled. "Crush it."

Cringing at the residents likely watching us from behind, I yanked into the mossy green of Dur-Alf and slammed a two-foot-wide crushing spell down onto the metal. It surprised me how easily it flattened, barely tugging at the posts while ripping the cross sections from them. With a short leap, I cleared the debris and trotted into the brush on the other side.

The wooden stable on Dahlia's property had well maintained brown panels, and the scent hinted at their occupancy. A startled snort came from inside, but I focused on the garage ahead rather than on the horses. I hadn't considered the noise they might make. If they'd been left for five days without care, they'd be nearly dead from dehydration. I'd taken care of my friend's horses enough in my childhood to be concerned.

From the corner of the barn, the distance to the garage door was about fifty feet. A single dark window stared at us midway down the wall beside the paneled door. Two windows were empty on the second floor. Taking a deep breath to push down the tightness in my chest, I threw a detection spell from Haven at the garage and tugged at Dur-Alf in case something had been left on the lawn.

Two horses in stalls lit with ghostly Haven white, but the path appeared clear. Marie and David were close behind based on their footsteps as I sprang across tan grass. At the door I made out a pale halo of a human, or humanoid shape, inside the house. Two. One appeared to be sitting at the front of the house, and the second sat deeper, where I imagined the kitchen or stairs from the layout.

I raised two fingers and turned, surprised to find Marie so close. Gesturing, I tried to point out where I saw the figures. She fixed me with a firm gaze, then focused on the door.

My veins throbbed in my neck as I dug into crumbling Dur-Alf to check for wards at the door or just inside the garage, then Mer to unlock the door. A tiny glimmer of liquid blue flickered at the top of the door jamb, and I stopped to inspect the ward. The runes were Nordic, and it took a moment to recognize a lifting spell. I'd never seen anything like it, but I motioned Marie back before working at it with my own lifting spell. I disrupted the sigil easily with one twist of a rune. They'd been marked with white pen on white paint. We'd have to be careful. Few used Mer as wards; they were unreliable.

I unlocked the door, but whispered before turning the knob. "The entries could be alarmed. If anyone moves inside, I'll unlock the next door as quick as I can."

David already had his weapon pulled and bobbed his head back and forth impatiently. We'd talked this all through on the ride. Marie rolled her eyes up from the door and studied me.

"Well, here goes." I turned the knob, stepped over the threshold, and tugged at Dur-Alf.

There were no visible wards.

The garage had an old red Fiero parked near the front and reeked of the dead golden retriever near the workbench at the back. Flies buzzed as David darted inside. The entry notification beeped inside the house.

"Move it," growled Marie.

I followed close behind him and tossed an unlocking

spell across the garage to the inner door before David reached it. A small heartbeat of relief passed when I did not spot a Mer sigil guarding it. The shape by the front window rose, alerted to our presence. Even as David closed the distance to the door in a flash, the occupant moved toward the other person, or creature, in the main area.

As David opened the door, I tugged another detection from Haven and the figures inside lit up clearly, appearing human though the farthest away did not move. I clamped my teeth down at the thought of a shrapnel vest.

I hadn't breathed since smelling the dog's remains.

Inside the main house, the yellow glow of lamps lit the doorway beyond the laundry room. Paintings adorned the walls along a staircase leading up to the right. David raced out of my sight, firing immediately toward the figure at the front.

As she stepped into the laundry room, Marie's tail formed out of liquid gold at her feet and wrapped around her thigh to dart ahead. The realm of Salmhalla and the emerging appendage moved unnaturally with her, like a portal into her world centered directly under her.

Haven flashed bright white inside the room, but not the level the lich had unleashed, more like an activated sigil. Perhaps the arcane user had gone invisible. David yelled and fired dully three shots in a row.

I came in behind Marie to find him dangling in the air, wrapped in Haven with a Dur-Alf shield tucked around him in a globe. Pausing at the exit of the laundry room, I noted half a dozen Dur-Alf wards lit across the floor and carpets.

The motionless figure on the far side of the room was Dahlia Roberts, based on the photos Tomas had sent. Likely wrapped in a binding from Dur-Alf, she sat stiffly at a dining table with a glass of water in front of her. Her couch and furniture were mainly cream and gray colors, giving the high ceiling room a sense of elegant expanse. The black sigils drawn into the cushions, carpet, and tile stood out sharply.

The laughing pale man who dashed behind her fit the description of the driver of the red corvette who'd likely turned Jenny into a zombie. He had three tan clay disks in his hand and barely gave me a leer before he threw one at Marie like a frisbee, cackling with a maniacal glee as he did so.

She'd been skirting toward the front of the residence, past the entryway. Marie's tail was trapped firmly in a shield and writhed, scraping against tile. She aimed her weapon at him, but didn't fire with the elderly Dahlia in front of him.

I jumped toward her and tried to stop the disk with a hasty lifting spell, but I was too late. When the clay hit the floor clattering to pieces, it broke the sigil, activating a Dur-Alf crushing spell which smashed Marie to the floor. Panic washed over me as I remembered the moment when her bones had been crushed.

David grunted and struggled against the high ceiling, and Marie wriggled helpless on the tile with a soft grinding noise. Dahlia aimlessly stared at the table in front of her. With a toothy white grin, the arcane user shifted his focus on me.

I threw two spells out simultaneously. The first was a lifting spell from Mer meant to pry between the tile floor and the edge of the crushing spell pinning Marie down. Sigils, arcane magic, had limitations in adaptability whereby a witch could refine a spell. If I could give Marie some space, she might be able to squeeze out. It appeared to be working, as she edged an elbow toward my spell.

I spun a binding spell from Dur-Alf around the shield

trapping her tail, over Dahlia, and onto the nearly unmoving arcane user. It slid off uselessly, likely due to a ward on his person or clothing. He laughed heartily, as if I had unleashed some joke.

I didn't want to kill him; we needed information. I pulled my own crushing spell from Dur-Alf, prepared to stop him so I could save Marie.

A disk fell in a soft arc past my face. I hadn't seen him toss it, but the spell on Marie had caught my attention for too long. I lurched to the side, toppling an entry table and lamp. If I kept to the edge of a crushing spell, I might have a chance.

The clay cracked at my feet, and I pushed away, grimacing in anticipation of the weight of Dur-Alf against me. Instead, the world sparkled gray for a flashing moment, then darkness engulfed me.

EIGHTEEN

The sounds around me changed with the beat of my heart. My pulse pounded in my ears, unheard a moment before. I blinked against utter darkness — a complete absence of light. As I shifted to rise, my fingers pushed into dusty dirt akin to ash, not cool tile.

Something to my left sniffed. It wasn't Marie. I froze. David's grunting and Marie's scraping on tile were gone, but there were fainter noises around me like a breeze brushing against rocks.

I half swallowed, stopping at the noise I made.

This is Tarus. Cold flushed up my neck.

Jade's prediction had come true. I didn't know what spell the arcane user had unleashed. Perhaps he'd summoned a cryptid — one which might be beside me now.

I felt exposed in the pitch blackness. The light inhale could have been a shout to my ears. Picking up my right hand off the ground, I reached for my holster.

The nearby sniff repeated, and a foot, a hand, or something shifted against the ash.

My hand paused at my side, touching my jacket and a loose chain. The amulet which could make me invisible. Were I not terrified, I would have laughed aloud. The most useless talisman one could have in Tarus where sight had no place.

Still, it drew me, as futile a comfort as it might be. Digging fingers into my pocket, I pulled out the long chain and pendant. I draped it over my head with one hand.

Nothing changed, but I hadn't expected it to.

I drew in a breath and stopped. There was little I knew about Tarus itself, except those who entered, or even touched it for more than a scrape, became a vampire. *Infected*.

Urgent panic tightened my muscles and skin. There were exceptions, and I didn't feel different, tainted, or infected.

I needed to get back. A witch could move between realms, though I never had. All were forbidden for humans, except Haven where there was no one and nothing. To transfer you had to be able to touch the realm, hold it, and pull yourself inside. I couldn't touch Earth.

Jade's description nearly derailed me. I had been screaming in pain, dying to her. More than anything else, I did want to scream.

Six realms touched Tarus: three of them that we knew were Earth, Haven, and Ya Keya. Ya Keya turned humans to werewolves. I didn't know Earth, and I didn't have time to experiment.

I reached for Haven with both hands. The misty white of the realm became a beacon in the black of Tarus.

Two paces away, a creature turned toward me with black eyes the size of saucers. Shaped like a long-legged lizard with the size and proportions of a deer, it opened a glistening mouth and sniffed. An impossibly long tail arced over its body and stabbed between the two glowing wisps of Haven, lodging into my Kevlar vest.

I screamed and dropped Haven as I jerked back. Already on my one knee, I fell flat.

Tarus exploded with cries of alarm around me. Groans and growls echoed in the air. Heavy footsteps vibrated the dust under my back. They were all coming for me.

Claws grabbed my boot, and nails pierced leather and scratched against the inside of my arch. Shrieking, I kicked something soft with my other heel and tried to propel myself away with the palms of my hands.

Jade's words haunted me. I couldn't die here and leave her alone.

Ignoring the roar only a pace or two from my right, I grabbed onto bright Haven and held.

The light lit the terror around me. A draugr had caught the lizard-deer, twisting claws into soft flesh. Gravel flesh reached for me with fingers the thickness of my thighs and a body so large it turned to shadow beyond the muscled arm.

Yelling at the realms, I pulled Haven over me like a cool misty blanket.

I cried as the bright light engulfed me and I pulled my body into a weightless fog.

Twisting and floating, my heart raced as if expecting a draugr's claw to reach through the nothingness from Tarus. I whimpered and breathed short breaths in and out, but there was nothing to fear in Haven. Legends abounded, but every witch's accounts were the same. Omnipresent and omni-directional light shone on a world of weightless drifting fog.

My heart could not let go of the reflex for flight, and my brain still flashed horrid images. How had anyone ever survived Tarus?

I sucked in a breath of air as sweet as if a rain had just cleansed it. I was trapped here. Marie was on Earth being crushed by a Dur-Alf spell. Would she survive if I never made it back?

I couldn't touch Earth; I didn't know how. Jade had seen my death in Tarus, but it might end on Haven. A seer brushed all realms unwittingly. Too sensitive, my daughter had been cursed from an early age with realms constantly appearing. The shifting temporal swirls of Mer brought the future to seers like my daughter. The realm had to be touched without intent to provide such visions. Upon focus, Mer aligned with those who touched it. If Jade were here, she'd likely be able to see the Earth realm.

Floating without any sense of an impending fall, my pulse dropped to a steady beat as panic fled. I could not calm the tightness in my chest brought on by a desperate urgency to return to Marie — and my life back on Earth. Thirst thickened my throat, so I assumed I could easily die here in Haven. How had the witches who visited Haven returned to write about it?

I could hear my grandmother, Leyna, chastising me for not reading the tomes she'd collected. She had dedicated her later years to the study of the craft and realms. I'd learned much from her, but not enough, it seemed.

Her lessons had followed my mother's. The first we learned was how to find the realms. I could try that.

I stretched a hand out, focusing on my fingertips. Symbolic only, Leyna had said, but a place to start. Pushing against the fabric of the universe, not the air, I waited for colors and sensations to appear.

The liquid gold of Salmhalla flowed to the left of my middle finger, and I pulled back to keep from touching it. The dragons were very clear about the death which awaited any human who touched their realm. It might be a last resort.

Black Tarus glimmered near my index finger, and I again drew back, shivering.

According to accepted realm mechanics, each place touched six others, but not the same six. I had known Haven touched Salmhalla and Tarus — and Earth, but what were the other three? None had been listed for Haven that I knew of.

I drew a deep breath, hoping that the Earth realm would feel familiar to my eyes and senses. The description was likely in Tomas's database. Hopefully he'd get to tell me what an idiot I was for not knowing.

A chill crawled up my spine, and my breathing sped up. I'd been in Tarus. By everything I'd ever learned, it would be a miracle not to have been turned into a vampire. What did it feel like? Would I know?

Stretched out in front of my face, my hand trembled. If I turned into a vampire, David would never let me live it down.

Frowning, I focused on my hand, waiting for a hint of realms as I pressed again, willfully trying to touch the universe. Molten red, the color of fresh lava, showed near my thumb. I held close without fully touching it. Surely they would have made a memorable mention if Earth showed that brightly. Wetting my lips, I pressed into it and recoiled from the heat. It didn't burn my flesh, but my reflexes were as if touching a hot pan. The texture seemed like what I would expect from molten rock.

If realm mechanics were correct, I had two more realms to find: Earth and an unknown place. Finding the molten realm had given me some hope.

I pushed again, my eyes flicking from one finger to the next. Salmhalla and the molten realm appeared again, but

I did not touch them. I was biting my lip when I noticed a distortion near my pinkie's fingernail. The air wavered, like heat rising off hot asphalt. A bit too abruptly, I jabbed my pinkie into it. Thick brown mud appeared, rising cool around my finger.

What should I expect? Should Earth feel like home? I had enough of a touch to the muddy realm that I could grasp some of it or even dig in and hold it. What if I went someplace more like Tarus than Earth?

"I'll just grab Haven and come back here," I told myself aloud. My voice sounded strange, scratchy. Maybe it was just hearing it in Haven, but I really didn't want to be a vampire. "Move it, Kristen." Marie and David needed me.

I closed my eyes, then steeled myself and opened them. Nothing could be as bad a Tarus. Reaching out my other hand, I found the wavering air, then the cool muck. Holding my breath, I took a firm grip onto the realm and focused on Marie.

CHAPTER

NINETEEN

Pulling into the realm felt gooey, like I would be suffocated. I couldn't help but close my eyes. My nerves suddenly flashed like goosebumps everywhere at once, inside and out.

I popped into air. Blinking, I took deep breath.

Marie was to my right now, not my left. I'd found the Earth realm. Her tail had receded, and she barely appeared to squirm, now flattened against the floor. David still fought against his binding.

The cloud of Tarus continued to churn where I'd been standing. My pulse rose as the sparkling darkness appeared to have a shape inside it.

The arcane user had to be my first focus before he attacked me again. I spun, pulling a binding spell and a crushing spell from Dur-Alf. One or the other would pin him if I could get past his wards.

He stood to my left, chuckling and focused on Marie. In his right hand, he held one of his clay sigils, the left he leaned on Dahlia's shoulder. If she were simply bound by an arcane spell, she would know everything that was happening around her. I would have to be precise to keep from crushing her with Dur-Alf.

My binding spell wrapped around the arcane user, alerting him and nearly appearing as if it would hold before it slid off from his ward. Dur-Alf slammed on top of him, scattering his cap to the floor. His wards again protected him as my magic crashed to the floor around him.

He staggered back from Dahlia, bouncing against the railing of the stairs, scanning the area around me.

I stood near a small table with a laptop where he'd been sitting when we arrived. I was glad I wore the amulet and could be in the open.

The arcane user shrugged, smirked, and curled back his hand to toss his clay sigil.

A roar sounded from my right where Tarus roiled. I couldn't focus on that at the moment.

My thumb released the holster before I drew my weapon. Where my grandmother and mother had taught me magic, my dad had trained me on guns and puns. The force had taught me to always take two shots to the chest.

The arcane user had almost released his disk when I put the first bullet into his heart. His sigil flipped into the air, drifting lazily, but still aimed close to me. His eyes were wide in surprise. I put a second bullet an inch from the first as his eyes began to roll back.

My left-handed lifting spell from Mer caught the disk in midair.

I had already stepped back with my right foot to reorient for whatever was emerging from Tarus. In the corner of my eye, above the arcane user, I thought something dark moved in a doorway at the top of the stairs. My jaw clenched, but I already tugged at Haven. It could have been a shadow of light or something else here in the house with us.

A ghoul's misshapen head and torso appeared, but it focused on Marie, the closest flesh. Unlike the intelligence of a draugr, the cryptid's dull eyes had only one interest: food. I tried not to think that this had been near me when I'd fallen into Tarus.

My first bullet hit the blotchy, gray chest and caused it to stagger back. Stretching a wide, full mouth of sharp teeth, it bellowed a terrifying scream but never took its eyes off Marie. I aimed lower for the second shot, and the miasma of Tarus faded and took the partially emerged ghoul with it.

Shifting my position by dropping my left foot back, I tossed a Haven detection to the top of the stairs as I stepped closer to Marie. Despite the dead man behind Dahlia, the arcane magic had not been broken. His wards still covered the room.

Dahlia glowed brightly, but nothing else showed above her on the second floor. I scanned quickly, then turned to Marie, keeping my weapon ready. The scent of spent gunpowder hung heavy in the air.

An arcane ward used as a trap requires it be broken to release, but the runes remain etched into the realm magic. In time, they will wear out depending on the sigil. I tugged at Dur-Alf, highlighting the crushing spell in a translucent dark green. Using the slightest crushing spell of my own, I broke the rune and disrupted the sigil, freeing Marie.

She rose slower than I expected. "Night storms. What the hell happened?"

I glanced at David, who had stopped struggling and stared down at us. His hat had fallen off his head but hung in the spell. "He used a crushing spell on you."

"Dancing monkeys, I know that." Marie gestured to

her own chest. "Take off the damn amulet." She pointed to where I'd fallen into Tarus. "You disappeared. The amulet?" Marie focused on Dahlia. "Never mind, we'll talk about it later. Did you have to kill him? I needed to know . . ." She didn't finish and shook her head. "Thank you. Are we clear?"

I winced in embarrassment as I holstered my weapon, took off the amulet, and tucked it into my pocket. I hadn't appeared invisible to myself, so it was easy to forget. "No. The room is heavily warded." I pointed at David. "Do you want me to get him down first or clear the room?"

Marie rolled her eyes and gestured to David. "Him, then room. And I want a full report after when we're alone. We'll have to be careful with her."

I studied Dahlia as I moved past Marie, closer to David. "Agreed." The woman could be compelled. I'd want to confirm the house wouldn't blow up before I released the binding.

It took a couple spells to drop David to the floor. I should have tried to cushion the fall, but I was drained. I'd have to be careful disrupting the other sigils.

As David stood, he picked up his hat and brushed it off. "I thought you might have ended up in Tarus, but I guessed the amulet."

I ran my tongue across my teeth, then leaned in and spoke quietly, knowing it would go over the comms. "Well, how do you know if you're a vampire?"

"Dashing good looks. Unless of course you let a dwarf bandage you up." Even with the sunglasses on, I knew he glanced at Marie. "You'd know. The myths are — exaggerated. Keep it to yourself."

I let out a long breath and began clearing a path to Dahlia. The glow of Haven had faded by the time we reached her. From her smell, she'd been left to sit for long periods without being released. If it had been five days fully bound, she'd be dead. In her light dress we were sure she wasn't wired to explode, and her open hands held no detonators.

"Release her," Marie finally said.

The moment I broke the spell, the woman staggered up from her chair. Her voice was a husky whisper, laced with rage. "Bella and Grande. He left them in the barn without water for the past two days."

I caught her as she started to fall. "Sit. Sit. We'll take care of them."

Her arm shaking, she reached for the water which had been sitting in front of her. "Fucking worm." Before Dahlia reached the glass, she pulled away from me and stumbled toward the arcane user who I'd shot.

Blood had pooled around him and soaked into his shirt. The two holes had bled to a larger single stain on his chest.

She held onto me for support as she kicked his shin. "Fucker. Killed Hopper right in front of me."

I assumed that was the dog in the garage. As she tried to get closer for more kicks, I pulled her back and gestured toward the water. "Drink. We're going to have a medic look at you." I glanced at Marie who nodded.

Dahlia let me offer her the glass. "Who the fuck are you clowns?" She waved her free hand at the room then David. "I'm old, not senile, and some crazy shit has been going on."

Marie responded as if there hadn't been magic and dragon tails in Dahlia's living area. "Special Agent in Charge, Marie Pyre of the FBI. Did you know the man?"

I took pictures of the arcane user and sent them to Tomas, hoping for an identification.

"No." The old woman drained the glass. "I've got to

see to my horses. Then . . ." She sagged as the bravado left her.

Marie gently coaxed the woman to sit. "David, get the horses some water. Kristen, sweep the area."

I worked my way across the room, discretely dismantling wards, before I headed upstairs. The first room I checked was where I'd seen the shadow. The sun hung low over the horizon and a tree near the house played with the light against the wall beside the door. There was nothing else unusual upstairs except wards at the windows. Finn and Tomas were coordinating clean-up and a forensic search by the local FBI along with transports for Dahlia. I had to wonder what the Consociation would do with her.

As I headed back to the stairs, David spoke with someone below. Two attendants in EMT uniforms led an irate Dahlia to the front door. With his handsome features wrapped in gauze, his charm had no effect with the two women and certainly none with the elderly victim.

Marie stared down at the dead arcane user. She spoke after the front door closed. "I really wanted to ask him some questions."

"Sorry." I would have liked the answers as well, but I was too tired to be upset. Warded as he was, I doubted I could have bested him in the lair he'd built. Finn and I together would have been different. "Based on the ammo order, it sounds like he had this planned for over a week."

Tomas spoke over the comms. "Your arcane user was Tim Lutwig. He's an activist for an Iliodor group."

I frowned, waiting for Marie to respond. My legs were tired, and I had no energy left, certainly none to argue.

"I know you'll disagree, but I believe Iliodor was behind this. It's over — for now." She watched as I sat on the last step of the stairs. "You were in Tarus and made it back to Earth. That's — impressive. How?"

"I pulled myself into Haven." Weary, I lifted my hand and pressed lightly at the universe, searching for the Earth realm. Light wavered around my index finger, then I dug into cool brown mud. "I found the Earth realm there." I needed to call Jade.

CHAPTER

TWENTY

Four hours later, I texted Finn as Marie and I pulled into the hotel parking lot. "Dɪᴅ ʏᴏᴜ ᴀɴᴅ Gᴀʀʏ ɢᴇᴛ ᴀ ꜰʟɪɢʜᴛ ʏᴇᴛ?" I'd check in on them if I could.

"Oɴ ᴛʜᴇ ᴡᴀʏ ᴛᴏ ᴛʜᴇ ᴀɪʀᴘᴏʀᴛ. Wᴇ ʟᴇᴀᴠᴇ ɪɴ ᴀ ᴄᴏᴜᴘʟᴇ ʜᴏᴜʀs."

"Sᴇᴇ ʏᴏᴜ ʙᴀᴄᴋ ᴀᴛ ᴛʜᴇ ᴏꜰꜰɪᴄᴇ."

"Yᴇᴀʜ. Hᴏᴡ ᴀʀᴇ ʏᴏᴜ ᴅᴏɪɴɢ?"

"I'ᴍ ʙᴇᴀᴛ ᴀɴᴅ ᴛʜɪɴᴋ ᴡᴇ sʜᴏᴜʟᴅ ʙᴇ sᴇᴀʀᴄʜɪɴɢ ꜰᴏʀ sᴏᴍᴇᴏɴᴇ ᴏʀ sᴏᴍᴇᴛʜɪɴɢ ᴇʟsᴇ, ʙᴜᴛ ɢʟᴀᴅ ᴛᴏ ʙᴇ ʜᴇᴀᴅɪɴɢ ʙᴀᴄᴋ." I'd actually argued against leaving with Marie.

"Lᴇᴀʜ ᴡɪʟʟ ᴏʀɢᴀɴɪᴢᴇ ᴀ ɢᴏᴏᴅ ꜰᴏʟʟᴏᴡ ᴜᴘ ᴛᴏᴍᴏʀʀᴏᴡ."

Marie pulled into a parking space and shut off the engine. "Fifteen to meet back out here."

David rattled his mints and opened his door.

"Wᴇ'ʀᴇ ʙᴀᴄᴋ ᴀᴛ ᴛʜᴇ ʜᴏᴛᴇʟ. Tᴀʟᴋ ᴛᴏ ʏᴏᴜ ᴛᴏᴍᴏʀʀᴏᴡ."

"Wᴇ'ᴠᴇ ɢᴏᴛ ᴀ ʟᴏᴛ ᴛᴏ ᴛᴀʟᴋ ᴀʙᴏᴜᴛ."

I smiled, assuming he meant Tarus and my return to

Earth. Marie watched me as I climbed out. "We'll have you home soon." She appeared undamaged from the crushing spell. A human would have been badly bruised.

"How are you doing?" I asked.

She slowed, letting us walk together. "Sore. You did well today."

"Well, I'd been pretty useless the rest of the day." Warming at her words, I appreciated the compliment.

"Not true. And I could have been more — precise." David had reached the doors and glanced back. Marie studied me. "You've still got concerns."

"I do. You know I don't think this was Iliodor, and even if Tim Lutwig had connections with the witch, someone compelled the others and possibly him as well." My exhausted brain spun through the list of people who had died. Marie would believe Iliodor responsible for them as he'd certainly caused similar carnage, but he'd never connected to Tarus. "Did Tim Lutwig have any reason to want you dead?"

"No. Never heard the name before."

David waited for us in the lobby, gathering stares from the two employees at the reception desk. We all appeared a little haggard.

I called Jade from my hotel room, unsure if she'd answer this early in the day.

"Mom?"

"Hey, Honey." I left the phone on speaker as I packed what little I'd left. I would have used lifting spells if I had any energy. "I needed to call you and let you know it's over. It happened, just like you said, but I'm okay. When I visit, I'll tell you the whole story."

"You — you're okay?" Her voice pitched as she began to cry.

"I'm perfectly fine. Not a scratch. I've got a hole in my boot." I smiled weakly and peered down, tilting my foot.

"I was so scared." Her words broke with light sobs.

Exhausted, my throat thickened with emotion. "I'm headed back home now. Can I call you tomorrow? I just wanted you to know so you could stop worrying."

"Okay, Mom."

Eyes blurry, I finished packing and met the team back at the Hummer. I barely noticed the ride back to the airport and curled around my Supernatural backpack in my lap. Between David and my excursion into Tarus, an unusually rank scent hung inside the Hummer. The petroleum aroma at the airport was a welcome break. When we got into the air, I slept on a plane for the first time in my life.

David had shed his gauze, hat, and glasses by the time I awoke with the jet in descent for a landing. His face had an angry red outline where the skin had been peeled off. Offering a lopsided smile, he spoke. "Didn't get a chance before, but thanks for not leaving me floating on the ceiling."

"Were you hanging on my every word?"

He tilted his head and winced. "I think you used a bullet."

"Waiting to get a drop on them?"

"That would be beneath me."

"Your comment went right over my head."

Raising her hand against both of us, Marie frowned then spoke. "I was hoping to take a day, but Stacey wants reports. Take your time, but I'll need you in tomorrow."

A little after 10:00 p.m., I climbed into my musty-smelling Chevy Cavalier and promised myself a new air freshener or a good cleaning. The trip from the airport was slightly farther than the FBI office, but not too much more.

Atlanta was never really quiet, but the ride was smooth and short, and no one had taken my parking space when I got to the apartment complex. Sometimes, if I was gone a couple days, they'd assume it vacant.

The stairs taxed my legs, and as hungry as I was, I considered eating just a quick yogurt and heading directly to bed.

"Kristen!" Astrid called from the parking lot. I hadn't even noticed her ride pulling into the complex to drop her off.

I leaned against the railing and stopped, three steps from the second-floor landing. My go bag hung from my shoulder along with my purse, and both felt like I carried rocks in them. In fact, I needed to refill my go bag. I waved with my free hand. On an easier night, I'd suggest a coffee before I binged on my art. Tonight, I barely forced a smile.

My tall blond neighbor had bright streaks of blue and purple that shone even under the dim lights of the parking lot. She wore a blue tank top and jean shorts which emphasized her knobby knees and elbows. She carried three grocery bags dangling off her arms and still spryly darted across the sidewalk.

I waited until she was at the bottom of the stairs to speak. "Hi, Astrid. Late night shopping?" We were friends, of sorts, but not being from the US, she had an odd view of things.

She started to respond, then squinted at me as she hopped up the stairs. Her gaze became more intense with each step. Astrid stopped, then tentatively reached out and touched my shoulder. Her eyes widened. "Are you okay?"

Memories of Tarus flashed in my mind along with the moment of helplessness in the barn and feeling stranded in Haven. "Rough day." My hair was likely wild, my shirt had a hole in the chest, and my face felt sunburned. It was no wonder she stared at me so.

Her lips pursed. "Which you can't talk about." She nudged me forward. "I've got a fresh baguette and brie. Let me throw this in my apartment and we'll take ten minutes. I can tell you're going to bed early tonight."

I wanted to just flop on my bed, but I should eat anyway. Besides, bread and cheese was never a bad thing. "Okay. I'll leave the door unlocked while I change into something loose." The reek of Tarus still hung in my clothes, even with the Kevlar vest off.

My apartment smelled like oil paints and fabric glue. Prior to this case, I'd been home a lot since the DRC had been quiet. I dumped bags, holster, and dirty clothes beside my bed and had pulled on a long t-shirt when the front door opened and Astrid called out, "It's me."

By the time I splashed water on my face and came out, she had sliced fresh French bread, found a cheese knife for the brie, and set glasses of water on my little dinette table. I was instantly starving. "Thank you. It's been a long day."

She flashed a smile and glanced at the food. "I wish you could tell me about all the places you've been, but I understand you can't."

I laughed. Tarus and Haven and back again. She'd think I was hallucinating. "Just North Carolina."

Astrid focused on slicing a piece of brie. "Seemed worse than that."

It had been. "Just a lot of running from here to there."

She handed me a wedge of cheese and bread. "But you made it home." From her understanding gaze, would she believe just how far I'd gone?

The next day, I woke mid-morning and hurried to work before lunchtime. Stacey had demanded via email that I report to her immediately in person, and I'd obviously not seen it. My reply explained that, but I still drove a little too fast.

Stacey's office was on a different floor, and I went directly there instead of checking in with Marie. I knew she'd understand.

I fussed with my curls as I entered the barren office. Stacey glared at me when I entered. "You're running late today."

There was no point in arguing. "Yes. Sorry. I'll get my report done in the next two hours."

She jabbed a finger at the chair. "Do you realize what a disaster your team has left? I've got five different offices demanding details that the DRC can't provide. We've only got so much sway among local agencies before I've got to pull in my superiors to squelch the noise."

"I don't know if it could have been helped." I didn't sympathize, because it was technically Stacey's job to use Consociation pressure in local government.

"It certainly could have. Your team blew up a barn. I understand you crossed over in front of witnesses and utilized a talisman."

I nodded, subconsciously tapping my pocket to reassure myself I'd brought the fancy amulet. "It was unforeseeable and not something we could control."

"I disagree. There will be an investigation. Make sure your reports are thorough." She pointed toward the door. "I'll expect them in an hour."

I stood, unsure why she'd had me sit at all. "I'll do my best." I'd dealt with similar bureaucracy before, but not with the Consociation. Marie would let me know what to expect for an investigation.

David sat at his desk in the middle of the row and glanced up when I entered. "It's totally rad you survived Tarus. Congrats. Shame no one will ever know." His face appeared to have healed more overnight to the point where only a few deeper areas were darker than his normally pale skin.

I didn't really want to discuss how terrified I'd been, at least not with David. I'd corner Finn at some point. "Rad?" I asked. "Is that like from the sixties or seventies?" I pulled out the White Diamond Periapt. "Did Marie say what to do with this?"

He shrugged and jabbed a thumb over his shoulder. "Make sure to knock."

I rolled my eyes and walked to Marie's door, making sure to open the door with some noise. "Hey, I finished with Stacey and wanted to check about this." I held up the amulet.

Marie peered over the top of her monitor. Her brown bald head had only a slight discoloration, though her eyebrows were still short from being singed. "The investigation? Don't worry about it. They are used to her games by now and come in and do a cursory review of reports, then leave. I'm surprised she didn't pull this for the last one." She pointed to her red and gold sofa, where her orange striped cat, Tiberius, lay curled at one end. "Sit. Tell me how you're doing. We talked a bit on the drive, but how are you feeling now that you've slept on it?"

I crossed the room and sat, letting Tiberius sniff my fingers before I scratched behind his ears. "I can touch Earth realm now." I hadn't gone into that detail on the ride.

"Be careful." Marie stood, catching Tiberius's attention.

"I know. Maybe the Consociation has someone who could train me?" Touching a realm did not mean you could control what it did. My mother and Leyna had painstakingly taught me the spells I did know. Luckily we had chickens, and I'd trained with, and destroyed, lots of eggs to get my spells right. From what I understood, Earth magic could be far more dangerous. I wasn't sure whether I wanted Herta, or possibly Tomas, to train me.

She stepped to the back of her office to the bookshelf that covered the wall. "I'll send out a request. It would be good have you trained when we can." Marie pulled out a brown leather tome. "Borrow this for a while to sate some of your other questions."

I put the amulet in my lap to take the heavy book with a simple title across the spine, *Walks Among The Undead*. I knew this as Rasputin's work. The inside title page marked it as translated and annotated. "Are you sure? Thank you."

"It might help you deal with the experience, or make it worse. One never knows." She returned to her desk. "You did good. I know I said it before, but I need you to stop second-guessing your place on the team."

Tiberius glared jealously at the book, and I shifted to continue petting. "I'm going to break up the reports to each scene. Do you want me to run them by you?" Finn had given my previous work a glance before sending them to Tomas and thus Stacey.

"You'll do fine." She pointed at the amulet. "First get with Tomas and get that to the Vault."

I flushed. "Does he know? Tomas?"

Marie chuckled. "Yes. Check in with him now."

Leaving my book on my desk, I held the amulet by the chain and walked back into the hall, turning right for Tomas's door. I waved instead of pressing on the keypad as Finn had done.

Not surprisingly, Tomas had a speaker hidden somewhere and managed to convey his annoyance. "Keypad."

I pressed my thumb on the pad, and the door clicked open. Hiding a mischievous grin, I entered the long hall with its sole flickering bulb. Pressing the second pad, I waited as the door clicked open and the aroma of popcorn wafted out. The monitors were all rolling with data streams, and I wondered what he was working on.

He spun his chair to face me. "The White Diamond Periapt?" he asked.

I was struck again by his gorgeous green eyes and long curly brown hair. His face was unnaturally handsome. I lifted the talisman. "Yep." My conversation skills diminished when confronted with beauty.

Tomas snorted and jumped off his chair with ease. His golden loop earrings swayed with the movement. "You know where the Vault is?"

"Yes." I probably had more words in my vocabulary, somewhere.

He waited, staring at me. "Can we get this over with?"

I startled into movement and pulled open the door to lead the way. No wonder he treated me like I was an idiot. "Sorry." My cheeks were warm, and I seriously considered wrapping the amulet in my palm to become invisible.

I'd cooled down by the time I let us into the ammo room and stepped aside at the Vault to let him take the lead. He wore a cream-colored buttoned shirt and tight-fitting brown slacks. As Tomas tapped three knocks on the door, I purposefully focused on his hair in case he turned around.

The same odd fog, seeming almost alive, rolled inside the entrance to the Vault. I followed Tomas in and closed the door. He smelled like nutmeg and salt. I barely noticed the glow at the far end or the Keeper's approach.

"Welcome, Keeper." Tomas bowed, rolling his head to the side as he did so.

The voice, reminiscent of Marie, responded from the darkness of the cowl. "Greetings, Tomas."

I swallowed and added my greeting when they paused. Tomas turned and glared at me, then at the amulet. "Oh, yes. I have brought you the White Diamond Periapt. For your care." When I stretched my arm forward, I brushed against Tomas, and the watery Mer realm flowed around him.

Tomas pulled back with such disgust that I felt cold inside. Didn't he have a human wife? Was it just me?

I barely heard the Keeper as he accepted the amulet. He was as careful as I to touch only the chain. When we finished, Tomas gestured brusquely for the door, and I slunk out ahead of him. I couldn't mention his behavior. However, when he glanced at me, I asked him a question. "What does Anka mean?"

Tomas frowned, "Dwarven for Dragon Saint." Stepping carefully around me, he sped for the door.

I emerged from the ammo room as he strode down the hall. By the time I got to our office, he'd already disappeared into his room. I'd asked Finn, but he hadn't believed Tomas disliked me any more than anyone else. Still, it felt personal.

I spent the afternoon feeding him reports on each scene, and it took well into three hours. Stacey would likely be upset, but I didn't think I could please her. Our little team accepted me, and that would have to suffice. I'd become comfortable here. There were still things I needed to resolve in my personal life, though; I would visit Jade this summer.

Marie strolled out a few minutes after my last report had been finished and I had started reading follow-up details from Leah. "Are you ready?"

I glanced from David to her. "For what?"

"Drinks. Dinner. Finn and Gary will meet us there."

David stood, straightening his jacket. "Bring a pen," he said.

I frowned as Marie bustled for the door. "Why?"

He smiled, handsome despite the lingering marks. "To sign his cast."

Grabbing Marie's book, I took the elevator down with them, but we all drove separately. I had planned on restocking my go bag, but it could wait.

When I arrived, behind both David and Marie, Leah had already joined the table, sitting beside Gary where I usually sat. She was pale skinned with dark eye shadow accenting bright blue eyes. Her blond hair was cut short in a bob just over her collar. Her long arm rested on the back of Gary's chair as she laughed at one of his jokes. A thick woven chain of platinum rings disappeared into a pale pink blouse.

She grinned when she saw me. "Kristen!" She patted the seat next to her. "I saved you a seat."

David usually sat there, but he'd moved to the end by Marie. Finn indeed did have a white cast stretched out next to Marie's chair. He flashed me a weak smile.

I maneuvered around David and sat beside Leah. She focused on my eyes and touched my arm. The gray mist of Ya Keya roiled around her. My eyes widened, and she laughed. I'd not known she was a werewolf.

"I promise not to bite," she said and gave me a full hug. "Finn told me you had quite the trip." Leah spoke quietly enough in my ear that Gary wouldn't hear. "We'll compare notes."

I swallowed, unsure if that meant she too had gone into Tarus. "Okay."

Gary winked at me and stroked his brownish gray beard in his hand when Leah released me. "I hear I owe you some thanks for getting Finn back in mostly one piece.

I knew I loved you for a reason." I was surprised how happy he seemed, considering the trouble they'd been having over Finn's job. He picked up a spoon and tapped his glass. "Finn has an announcement."

Finn's dreads danced as he shifted awkwardly, trying to sit up. "Yes. Pyre knows already, but I wanted to tell you all. I'm retiring."

My face slackened, though I couldn't be surprised. "Oh." He'd talked about it during the last case.

The server brought Marie one of her Loblolly beers, and I just pointed at it for my order. I'd grown accustomed to it. David ordered wine. I studied Leah. Was she Finn's replacement? I liked her, but I'd become close to Finn. We were both witches.

Marie waited for the server to leave. "Actually, I'm going to offer Finn a promotion instead."

Gary's eyebrows furrowed and he studied his husband. "I . . ." It sounded like he might argue the point.

She raised a finger. "It's a desk job. He'll coordinate some of our resources. Tomas is heavily tasked when we're live on a case, and Finn has a good mind for logistics. It'll help when we're not getting the support we should have with outside agencies. She raised her glass and toasted Leah. "Leah's been assigned to take on his field work."

Finn almost smiled, then peered at his husband. "We'll discuss it."

Gary rolled his eyes, but in a good-natured way. I could tell he'd agree. "It has possibilities."

Leah pinched Gary's cheek, then smacked my leg. Ya Keya flickered in my vision. I might enjoy having her as a teammate, especially if Finn were still at the office.

I smiled at Finn. "Well, we're going to need to find room for another desk."

AFTERWORD

I'm enjoying the DRC Files and excited to see you here at the end of Book 3. A quick thanks and a hope that you enjoyed this story, if you did then a review is always helpful.

Would you be interested in a free short from David's perspective? An incident in his past?

If you haven't read it already, you can download from BookFunnel a very quick read. It'll sign you up for a mailing list during the download, but it won't activate unless you confirm on the follow up email.

David's Journal #21 https://BookHip.com/FRQGMPM

Demon

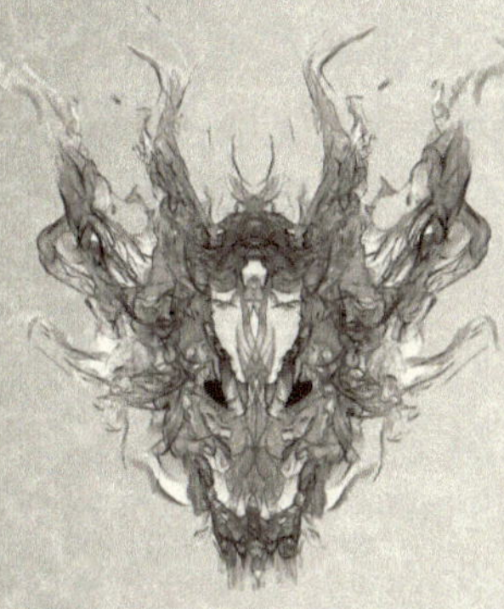

A demon is a rare inhabitant of the Tarus Realm who can be summoned to the Earth realm or cross of its own intent if given an opening. [1]

Their summoned forms often are a nightmarish mirror of their summoner with features designed to terrorize, such as claws, fangs, and horns. [1][2] Highly intelligent, they feed on strong emotions such as panic or rage. [2][3]

They are reported to rely on physical attributes for attack, but have been known to compel humans to act out their violence. [2][3]

(Cont. next page; Accounts of Demons in Tarus)

[1] Read Tinkanchtners's The Art of Demonic Summoning

[2] Read Kizurra's Referene on Tarus Cryptids Page 26 to 47

[2] Read Carey's Of Demons and Jinns

Dragon-shifter

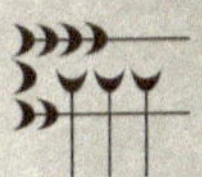

The portion of a dragon exposed in the Earth realm which can mimic the aspect of a human.

Most of what is known about dragon-shifters has come from archaic grimoires with questionable translations. [1][2] There is at least one resident on Earth to coordinate with the Consociation. [3] Reportedly, a dragon-shifter is an exact replica of a human, unless they intend otherwise. [2][4] A witch would know on contact.

The details of their craft ability are shrouded in myth due to their self-expulsion from the Earth realm prior to the Akkadian wars was preceded by a slow withdrawal during the prior era. [1][2][4] They openly apologize for their interference with man, resulting in the rituals that brought about the vampires and werewolves. [3][5]

(Cont. next page; Role in Consociation)

[1] Read Yin's Volume IV of Realm Studies Pages 1340 to 1489

[2] Read Wooley's Anecdotal Studies of Salmhalla

[3] Read Ferno's Presentation of the Consociation

[4] Read Inhai Du Anya's Scriptures of the High Dragons Page 1-72

[5] Read Sover's On Madness

Draugr / Draughr

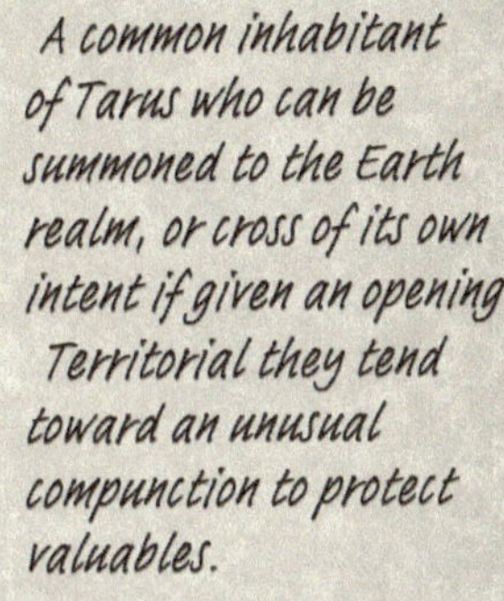

A common inhabitant of Tarus who can be summoned to the Earth realm, or cross of its own intent if given an opening. Territorial they tend toward an unusual compunction to protect valuables.

Tall and strong they present as humanoid on Earth with no skin and sharp black nails. They possess reflexes and speed beyond humans.[1] Savage and instinctual on a physical level. Relatively low intelligence.

Magical or Arcane abilities: None

Note the Akkadian ritual listed in the 1911 appendix

[1]Read Macrin's Journal for an in-depth biological reference compilation of Merfolk research of the Draugr

Dwarf / Dwarves

Humanoid residents of Dur-Alf with a proclivity for exploration and research. Their earliest interactions with humans caused a wider disturbance than expected and their own sanctions for crossing to Earth were ignored by many of their more independant scholars and explorers. Brief conflicts existed between individuals as witches developed the ability to pass into the Dur-Alf realm.

Small in mass and stature, their biology is similar to Earth mammals. [1]

Conflicts erupted between humans and dwarves [2] as human witches and arcane users began to cross realms. Dwarves are especially biased against vampires.

(Cont. next page; Magical and Arcane usage)

[1] Read Maorin's Understanding Dwarven Physiology and Psyche

[2] Read Thant's War on Human Mutation

Kuru Kuru

Mammallian bipedal residents of Dur-Alf though the only known description of their physical resemblance comes from two sources and both differ slightly. [1][2]

The Dwarves do acknowledge their presence and the Kuru Kuru have been given access to the Consociation. [3] They speak only to the Dragon delegation there and have some relationship with Dragons. [4]

Small in mass and stature, their biology is similar to Earth mammals with a flattened muzzle. Reports differ on fur (pictured), or with feathers. [1][2][3]

(Cont. next page; Magical suppositions)

[1] Read Kainin's *Guide to Dur-Alf, Eden of the Realms*

[2] Read Emily Randolp's *Memoirs Among the Sprites*

[3] Read Daesalu's *Biography of Talat*

[4] Read Ono Seyo's *Conspiracy of the Consociation*

Merfolk / Mer

   Mer, called Merfolk by the Consociation, have the ability to transform into similar mammalian shapes upon interrealm movement. [1]

   Little is known about their unaltered form except that it is a sea mammal of some type, hypothesized to be porpoise-like. [2]

   Their longstanding habitation of Earth's oceans ceased at the point when Earth witches and arcane users began using the Mer realm in magic which coincided with the interrealm movement of humans to Dur-Alf. [3] Merfolk returned to Earth during the formation of the Consociation at the urging of the dwarves with whom they had long enjoyed diplomacy and trade. [4]

   Many Mer research and work on Earth as part of their proposal to the Consociation for admittance. [5]

(Cont. next page; the impact of Merfolk on magical use by witches and the arcane)

[1] Read Sienna's Treatise on Earth's Devastation

[2] Read Tino Vangian Biography of Venis: Traitor of Mer

[3] Read Sienna's Treatise on Mer Isolation

[4] Read Tino Vangian Biography of Venis: Traitor of Mer

[5] Read Tino Vangian's Biograpy of Sienna

Revenant

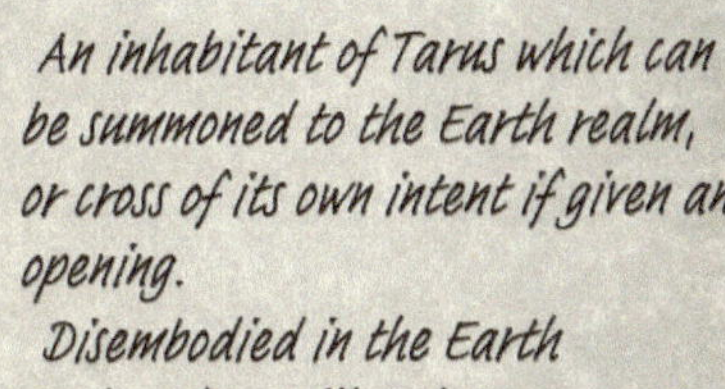

An inhabitant of Tarus which can be summoned to the Earth realm, or cross of its own intent if given an opening.

Disembodied in the Earth realm, they will seek to possess a humanoid corpse, or living entities with a weakened consciousness such as comotose or those near death.

Their corporeal control depends greatly on their prior experience. [1]

They range in intelligence and will avoid confrontation where possible.

Expellation is relatively simple depending on the skill of the witch. [2] Vampires have an innate ability to remove Revenants from their possessed hosts.

Magical or Arcane abilities: None

[1]Read Rasputin's Walks Among the Undead for a detailed observance of summoned Revenants

[2]See Appendix from 1892 - reference Possession

Vampire

A vampire is a human-born crossover to the Tarus realm. They are infected with a Tarus symbiotic life form initially misunderstood as a form of magic inherited from Tarus. [1] The infection can be summoned, gained through prolonged contact with Tarus, or transferred by blood-to-blood transfer with a vampire. [2]

The human cells are mutated to a far more resilient state and can be controlled to an extent which allows the vampire to change facial features and extend their life. [1] [3] Strength and speed are are increased with minimal muscular and bone alterations. [4] Vampires are entirely resistant to infection, disease, and toxins. [3] Mental acuity does not change. Emotional reactions remain, though extended life spans have brought interesting results. [1] [3] [4] [5]

(Cont. next page; the Tarus symbiote)

[1] Read Tonsun's *Illuminating the Mystery*

[2] Read William Beckett's *Becoming a Legend*

[3] Read Annan's *Study on Mutation*

[4] Read Anonymous *Confessions of Self-Hatred*

[5] Read Macrin's *Sapien Emotive Reponses* Pages 21-88

Werewolf / Dreamer / Hunter

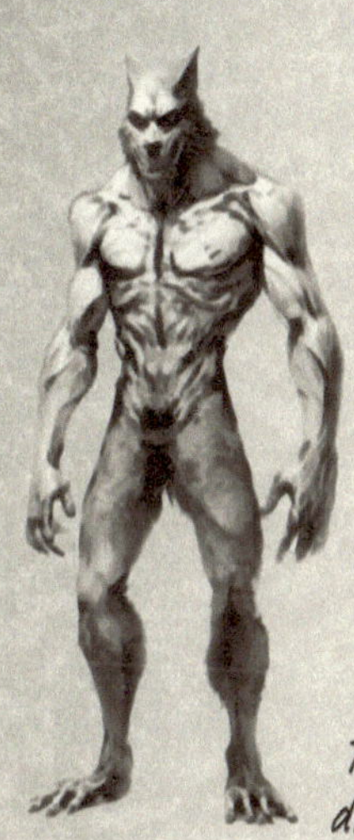

Born human they have developed a psychic and realm connection to Ya Keya. They are affected by their interactions and develop biological alterations. The connection can be summoned, by a ritual interaction with the bodily fluids of a mature werewolf, or through intense submersion in Ya Keya. [1] Longevity varies [2]

Transmuted form:
They gain 15-20% more mass directly from the Ya Keya realm. Reflexes, strength, and speed increase by 10-30% beyond their human norms. Eyesight and hearing are more acute though more age dependant than other attributes. [2]

(Cont. next page; loss of Magic and Arcane usage)

[1] Read Kizurra's History of Akkadian Werewolves - the Dawn

[2] Read Demot's Monograph for an in-depth biological reference

Dur-Alf

Visible indications are a dark-green color and a crumbling or dusty consistency.

Dur-Alf is a planet realm similar to Earth in that it orbits a singular star; it is the fourth of eight known bodies in the system and does not have any satellites. There are major land-locked bodies of water and large polar ice caps. [1] Rivers and lakes abound in most regions except near equatorial deserts. The seasons are mild, and wildlife is plentiful. [1] [2] The only known transplants from Earth are kestrels and a variety of water birds including swans, geese, ducks, and kingfishers. [1] [2] [3]

Humans are no longer welcome or tolerated in the Dur-Alf realm. [4]

Known bordering realms: Earth, Mer, Salmhalla, Mer, and Tique (described as a hostile realm [5]).

(Cont. next page; Known Species)

[1] Read Kainan's *Guide to Dur-Alf; Eden of the Realms*

[2] Read Emily Randalp's *Memoirs Among the Sprites*

[3] Read Yin's *Volume VI of Realm Studies* Pages 1289 to 1402

[4] Read *Consociation Guidelines for Interrealm Treaties*. Page 157.

[5] Read Yin's *Volume VIII of Realm Studies* Page 44 to 399

Haven

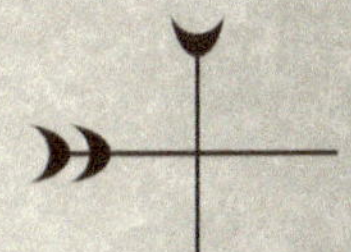

Visible indication is a white mist of a thick consistency reminding some observers of cotton candy.

Haven is a plane realm of breathable air, moisture in the form of clouds or mist, and no gravity. The ambient light is bright. No lifeforms or other identifying components have been found in the realm. [1][2][3]

Dwarves and Merfolk have often used Earth merely to experience the realm. [3][4] Other than the magic available by touching the realm, little of use exists there.

Hypothesises exist as to alternates states. [3][5][6]

Known bordering realms: Earth, Salmhalla, and Tarus.

(Cont. next page; Consociation Prohibitions)

[1] Read Yin's Volume III of Realm Studies. Pages 239 to 449 and appendix A

[2] Read Macrin's *A Bridge to Haven; the Trail of Tears and Tribulations*

[3] Read Innatala's *Forgotten Path*

[4] Read Soen's *Research on Haven*

[5] Read Ilionor's *Mystics Realm*

[6] Read Iai's *Casual Observances and Lost Myths*

Mer / Ishi-Iyai-Eyai-I 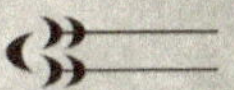

  Visible indication is a blue-green liquid of a denser consistency than water.

  Mer is a planet realm, a water-encased world with islands and some non-aquatic life. [1] Mer is the third planet from a hot star with higher than Earth surface temperatures and a single satellite. [2] Like Earth's humans, merfolk are the single indigenous intelligent life. Non-indigenous sentient life include the porpoises and whales, two of the numerous transplanted species between the two realms. [2]

  No reported excursions into the realm have survived, and the merfolk refuse access to the realm, part of their reasoning for joining the Consociation.

  Known bordering realms: Dur-Alf, Earth, and Tarus.

  Interrealm travel from Earth by humans is prohibited by the Consociation Regulations. [4]

(Cont. next page; historical connection to Earth and Dur-Alf)

[1] Read Sienna's Treatise on Mer Isolation

[2] Read Tino Vangian Biography of Venis: Traitor of Mer

[6] Read Consociation Guidelines for Interrealm Treaties. Page 114.

Salmhalla

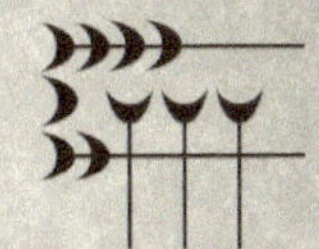

Indications include a liquid gold which is burning hot to the touch. [1]

Salmhalla is a plane of ambient sunlight and hot air temperatures. [1] [2] The plane contains a wide range of Earth-like terrains but predominantly includes mountains and grassy hills. [1] [2] [3] Several large water bodies have been detailed, but none rise to the level of oceans. [2] [3] [4] [5]

Consociation guidelines prohibit interaction with the realm and dragons enforce this edict. [6]

Known infringements have resulted in death, disappearance, mental illness, and loss of memory.

(Cont. next page; Known, theorized, and postulated magics connected to the Salmhalla realm)

[1] Read Yin's Volume IV of Realm Studies. Pages 1121 to 1349 and appendix C

[2] Read Inhai Du Anya's Scriptures of the High Dragons. Pages 89 to 97.

[3] Read Serjin's Testimonials

[4] Read Ilionor's Biography of Reshin. Pages 245 to 271.

[5] Read Wooley's Anectdotal Studies of Salmhalla

[6] Read Consociation Guidelines for Interrealm Treaties. Page 57.

Tarus

Visible indications are a dark-gray color and a misty consistency with glittering elements akin pin head .

Tarus is a plane realm with no ambient lighting and an oxygen-rich atmosphere. [1][2] Theories vary that the indigenous lifeforms have abilities to perceive lower frequency magnetic waves, have other senses, or solely rely on tactile and auditory senses. [2][3][4] Most grimoires record little of verifiable evidence, but specimens from the realm have been studied extensively by multiple races. [5][6] A rocky, waterless terrain is a commonly accepted description. [2][4]

Known bordering realms: Earth, Haven, and Ya Keya.

(Cont. next page; Consociation Prohibitions)

[1] Read Yin's Volume II of Realm Studies. Pages 71 to 549 and appendix B

[2] Read Rasputin's Walks Among the Undead, the annotated version.

[3] Read Serjin's Agreements in Darkness

[4] Read Ilionor's Dedication

[5] Read Finyai's Tarus Biology

[6] Read Ted Dansworth's Research of Tarus Corporeal

Ya Keya 

 Indications include a light gray mist which is moist to the touch.

 Considered the hunter's dream world, it is a plane of blue gray twilight according to numerous excursions including a Merfolk expedition led by Antre.[1] The plane contains a wide range of Earth–like terrains but predominantly includes forests, plains, and savannahs. No large water bodies have ever been detailed, but marshes and bogs were noted. [2]

 Continued interaction with the plane consistently results in a transmutation on a cellular level and the werewolf's bodily fluids become contagious.[3] Longevity and increased metabolic functions have been studied extensively. [4] [5]

 Witches and Merfolk have lost all abilities to interact with the realms once transmutation has occurred.

(Cont. next page; Known Inhabitants of Ya Keya)

[1] Read Antre's paper on To Ya Keya: Sacrifice and Betrayal

[2] Read Yin's Volume III of Realm Studies

[3] Read Jayne Dunham's Voyage Home

[4] Read Kizurra's History of Akkadian Werewolves - the Dawn

[5] Read Demot's Monograph for an in-depth biological reference

ALSO BY KEVIN A DAVIS

Please head to my website and join my mailing list if you'd like to be kept up to date on this series or my other books.

DRC Files - An episodic paranormal procedural series

Book One: Atlanta's Guide to Cryptids

Book Two: Tallahassee's Manual on Arcane Artifacts

Book Three: Carolina's Handbook on Summoning

Find out more

Website KevinArthurDavis.com

Facebook @KevinArthurDavis

KevinADavis on Instagram

KevinADavisUF on Twitter

ACKNOWLEDGMENTS

I'm proud that April enjoys the DRC files since her proofing has caught a number of errors which would have gone to print. She's given me the encouragement to put my focus on this series. If you're looking forward to the next one, you have her to thank.

Robyn Huss, my editor, weaves words like an Aes Sedai uses magic. If you enjoy this, it's largely due to her. If you're a writer, I encourage you to look at some of the opportunities she offers - http://www.hussediting.com/

The Fireside Group; Tim, Siena, Rosemary, Mark, Vail, and Katharine keep me challenged to do better and let me brainstorm a lot of what I'm working on with them. Arrash and Michele from Jody Lynn Nye's DragonCon workshop keep me on task with the most intricate details and loving support. Dianne and Brett from Apex have been there for me.

I still miss David Farland's gentle mentorship. Please pick up one of his books and enjoy the magic he endowed upon the world. Writers, study his lessons at Apex Writers.

Jody Lynn Nye's Dragoncon workshop will always be my go to suggestion for an in-person critique for any aspiring writers. Her insight is invaluable.

Another suggestion for new and developing writers is the Authors Workshop Track at JordanCon where guests, including writers, editors, and publishers, work with authors directly.

Support creatives! The wonderful cover art is by MIBLart! Consider them for your next design.

Thank you.

About the Author

Kevin A Davis is an author from north Florida who travels the southeast United States to vend, speak, and sometimes just as a fan of nerdy conventions.

The AngelSong series and the Khimmer Chronicles are completed series which you can find in paper, audio, and digital. The DRC Files is an episodic series with no completion arc planned. Hopefully, you've enjoyed these books.

Reviews are helpful on Goodreads and Amazon, but especially by word of mouth to your like-minded friends.

Works in progress include a YA shifter romance and an Epic Fantasy series while episodes 4 of the DRC Files is completed and await its editor.

Please follow and find out more
  Website KevinArthurDavis.com
  Facebook @KevinArthurDavis
  KevinADavis on Instagram
  KevinADavisUF on Twitter
  @inkdpub on TikTok